Whops and Clobber

R Humphries

Woodettes Publications

Published 2009
by
Woodettes Publications
Houston, Texas, USA

© Woodettes Publications 2009

The Library of Congress has catalogued this edition as follows Humphries, R [date]
Whops and Clobber : a novel by R Humphries
1st Ed.

ISBN 978-0-578-02606-0

www.woodettes.wordpress.com

Author's Note

This is a work of fiction. Names, characters, places and incidents are either the product of the author's imagination or are used fictitiously. Any resemblance to actual events or locales or persons, living or dead, is entirely coincidental.

The stories based at the Woody Back to School Unit are works of adult fiction based upon the real-life fantasy games played by the author, R. Humphries and his wife, the inimitable Jojo.

It is the author's intent to create the Woody Back to School Unit as an imaginative world peopled with a believable cast and set in familiar surroundings within which the readers will become comfortable.

The vernacular used in the stories is a combination of the phraseology derived from writing such as the British penny comics from the nineteen thirties, current language, slang and idioms, and the invented parlance known as Woody Jargon.

As such references to 'beating', 'thrashing', and 'flogging' have no context to the use or avocation of physical violence, with the exception of controlled corporal punishment, against the characters of the stories.

**Dedicated
to
My Beloved Jojo**

Contents

Prologue

Six of the Best

Mr Humphries flexed the long, thin rattan cane between his hands. Across the other side of the room a straight-backed chair was placed in front of an over-sized fireplace. Beside the chair Joanna Heyworth was preparing herself to be caned.

Jojo, as she was known to her chums, leaned over the chair, placing her palms on the cushioned seat.

Mr Humphries placed the cane on a nearby desk and shrugged off his suit jacket. He rolled back the cuffs of his white shirt and then loosened his tie.

He crossed the room to where Jojo was stooped over the chair and reached down and took the hem of her skirt between his fingers. He meticulously turned the skirt up her back. Joanna pushed her hips away from the chair to allow him to roll her bumbags down to behind her knees.

Once her garments had been appropriately rearranged she leaned further forward, reaching down and grasping the cross-bar of the chair. Her head hung down between her arms and her red hair cascaded on the seat.

At twenty-six years old, and now six years into her sentence at the Woody Back to School Unit, it was a position with which Jojo had become intimately familiar.

Mr Humphries positioned himself, feet slightly apart, and tapped the cane down to get his precise measure. Jojo's buttocks twitched slightly at the feel of the cane against her naked flesh and she braced herself.

Mr Humphries sliced the cane through the air. As a consummate professional he didn't require a particularly long backswing, knowing that the real power came from a last minute flick of the wrist that would accelerate the shaft of the cane to an alarming speed.

The cane left a long, slender mark across the crown of Joanna's behind. Her body jerked a little but she stayed steadfastly in position.

Mr Humphries knew that the most effective technique was to space the strokes out, leaving a thirty second gap before delivering the next one. This allowed the full effects of the cane to be experienced by Miss Heyworth.

Jojo was experiencing the full effects of the lick of the cane. First the shocking flesh burn upon impact, which was quickly followed by the sting of the cane ricocheting around her central nervous system like a pinball and electrifying her nerve endings. Finally as she hung panting over the chair desperately trying to catch her breath the deep under burn would set in.

Mr Humphries smiled appreciatively as Jojo stuck her buttocks up. A really good caning is a partnership. It was Mr Humphries' job to make sure that he landed the strokes in the sweet spot of the upturned behind, avoiding wraparounds or high or low riders. It was Jojo's task to present the target as high and steady as possible.

Jojo winced as the cane sliced down again. She was desperately trying to get into the zone. "It's only whops, it's only whops," she repeated over and over in her head.

Mr Humphries was caning with expert precision. Every stroke was landing in the target area. Angry red stripes sat up like tramlines from the pale flesh of Jojo's naked derriere; she was beginning to twitch and squirm between strokes as the heat intensified.

The first five strokes were separated by millimeters, perfect lines running from left to right across the flesh.

Mr Humphries shifted his position slightly and raised the cane about twelve inches above Joanna's behind.

Jojo gritted her teeth, knowing what to expect. The cane sliced downwards cutting diagonally across the existing stripes, creating a perfect five bar gate. The pain was excruciating and she shook her head from side to side in consternation.

She hung upside down across the chair for a full minute while she collected herself. Finally she pushed herself up, reaching back and lowering her skirt, then reaching down and retrieving her bumbags. She turned around and faced Mr Humphries. Her face was pale but her eyes were dry.

"That," she told Mr Humphries emphatically, "is what I call six of the best!"

The New Grand Master

The inmates of the Woody Back to School unit were assembled in the Great Hall awaiting the arrival of Grand Dame Lawton. It was the first morning of their return from summer furlough and they were scheduled to spend the next thirteen weeks completing the next phase of their Extreme Social Rehabilitation programs.

The Brass arrived first; the fourteen Dames who acted as their tutors, instructors and wardens while they were resident at the facility. Once the Brass was seated on the stage Ms Lawton swept into the hall. As usual she was smartly dressed in a black suit, and a white on white long-collared blouse, worn open at the neck. Her make-up was immaculate and her hair perfectly coiffed. She was followed by a gentleman who was unfamiliar to the inmates.

He also wore a dark suit, crisp white shirt and a patterned tie. He followed Ms Lawton up onto the stage.

The Grand Dame remained standing, behind a large desk. She greeted the inmates courteously and welcomed the twelve newcomers who were starting their sentences of seven years at the facility, without the possibility of parole.

Ms Lawton removed her glasses and placed them on the desk. The experienced inmates exchanged knowing glances; this was generally a sign that the Grand Dame was about to embark upon a lengthy diatribe regarding the rules, regulations and protocols that dictated their lives while they were secured in the compound.

"I have an important announcement," she started, "as you are well aware, last year we imposed a zero-tolerance program known to all of you as Operation Scorched Arse. Upon reflection I now believe that the program was not as successful as I had hoped. I take full responsibility for the operation and as a result I have decided to give you the opportunity for a fresh start."

The inmates exchanged curious glances.

"I have decided to stand down from my position as Grand Dame," she said slowly.

There was a chorus of shocked gasps from all around the hall.

"It is my great pleasure to introduce Mr Humphries," she continued, "who will take over in the role of Grand Master with immediate effect."

The Brass and inmates gaped as Mr Humphries rose to his feet. He walked around the desk and casually hopped up and sat on it, his legs swinging and dangling.

"Good morning, ladies. My name is Humphries. Mister Humphries." He grinned. "I've always wanted to say that."

"I know that this will have come as a surprise to all of you and that it will take a little getting used to. Nonetheless, I am confident that once we have had the opportunity to meet both collectively and individually the transition will go smoothly."

"It is my intention to continue the Grand Dame's remarkable record of successfully socially rehabilitating you to the standards established by the Ministry of Extreme Social Rehabilitation," he told the startled audience. "I intend to make a number of revisions to the protocols that I believe will eliminate some of the harsher practices introduced last year while still ensuring that the administration of the facility remains consonant with security and good order."

He went on to welcome the new inmates to the facility and he assured the gals returning to continue their sentences that he intended to raise the bar in their achievement in academia, in sports and the arts and in technology. He spoke in a quiet, self-assured manner. He talked briefly about the benefits of team spirit and promised them that he would meet with them individually in the near future. He informed them that during the summer months he had established a new intranet system, known as GalGab, and that the revisions to the protocols would be posted during the next few days.

Then, quite casually the Grand Master slid off the table and wandered across the stage, disappearing behind a curtain, and then sauntering back, a slender thirty-six inch cane in his hand.

With a friendly smile on his face he returned to his seated position on the desk, and swished the cane through the air.

"Unpleasant little critter ain't it?" he said calmly. Then he laughed. With that he placed the cane on the table and smiled at the startled inmates. "I'll leave Ms Lawton to give her final address," he said casually and with his hands thrust in his trouser pockets he walked nonchalantly from the stage.

2

Goodbye, Ms Lawton

The Famous Four lounged about in Jojo and Nicola Jane Nixon's study.

"Seems ok," said Deborah Morton.

"Seems nice," agreed Jojo.

"Cool suit," grinned Nicola Jane.

"Bit of all right," chuckled Rosemary Booker.

After Ms Lawton had finished her farewell address she announced that Mr Humphries had decided that the start of the formal curriculum would be postponed until the following morning to allow the inmates time to get used to the idea of the new chain of command.

The study shared by Jojo and Nix acted as the social center for the gathering of the influential cult of inmates known as the mega-minxes. The cult had originally been founded by the notorious party-gal and Extreme Ladette, Cathryn Cassidy, who had authored 'The Manifesto of Mega-minxdom'. Over the years covert membership had boomed. Throughout the morning Jojo and Nixdown's chums congregated in their study to discuss and debate the remarkable turn of events.

"I wonder how Patty's going to take to having a new boss?" mused Jojo.

Patricia Hodge was the Deputy Grand Dame at the facility. Patty was apoplectic. The news of Ms Lawton's resignation had comes as a bolt from the blue.

"This is preposterous," she raged to Katie Beck and Dame Wharton. Katie acted as Matron to the facility and Ms Wharton was the Geo-Dame. Together with Patty they formed a group known as the Radical Right which was notorious for their stringent interpretation of the rules, regulations and protocols and their propensity for dispensing corporal punishment.

"I am next in line," Patty complained. "That bitch never even consulted me. I have a good mind to complain to the Ministry."

"That might be a little hasty," counseled her cohorts. "We don't know what the Grand Dame has told the minister about Operation Scorched Arse and you might not want him poking around in your business."

"Grrrrrrrrr!" growled Patty Hodge.

"How is Patty taking it?" asked the Grand Master.

"She's absolutely furious," said Susan Lawton.

"Just as you predicted," grinned Mr Humphries.

"She was terribly charming and wished me luck," laughed Ms Lawton, "but I've known her a long time and I know she can't be trusted. Unfortunately she's a necessary evil so you'll need to be careful."

"I'm used to necessary evils," sighed Mr Humphries, "I'll be watching her carefully."

"Yes, but, remember one thing about Patty," warned Susan Lawton. "She'll be watching you, watching her."

The Grand Master just smiled.

Susan Lawton placed the last of her suitcases in the trunk of her car. She turned back and took a last look at the familiar surroundings of the Woody Back to School compound. The huge rambling facility was set in sixty acres of downshire grounds. The main building was spectacular and imposing, four wings built around a columned quadrangle. There was a separate building known as the Great Hall, sumptuous stables, outdoor recreation areas and several tennis courts.

It was a walled community, some distance from town and safe from prying eyes.

It was ten years since Susan Lawton, a major in Military Intelligence with responsibility for 'special discipline', had been approached by the System, a dark and covert government agency, to establish the experimental unit to house the nations most Extreme Ladettes. The inmates were generally between the ages of eighteen and twenty-five and had been found guilty of contravening the government's civil disobedience laws known as anti-Ladetting. They would serve sentences of seven years without the possibility of parole.

Ms Lawton had made her name in the military while serving on the Court Martial commission. Tired of sentencing recalcitrant servicewomen to fruitless months in the brig she proposed that most of the cases could be satisfactorily resolved by a swift six of the best. She argued that women were born broad of beam and perfectly designed to absorb a good tight dose of the cane.

What became known in military circles as the Lawton Alternative proved a surprisingly popular solution amongst the more rambunctious elements of the services.

When she was approached by the Ministry of Extreme Social Rehabilitation to act as the Grand Dame of the new facility Susan Lawton drafted a proposal entitled 'Whops and Clobber'.

Ms Lawton proposed that the unit should be run along the lines of her alma mater, the Woody School, which had once had the reputation of being the strictest boarding school in the country. The inmates would participate in a structured daily curriculum of tutorials, artistic and sporting activities. They would wear uniforms known as clobber and the standard form of discipline would be corporal punishment.

Ms Lawton slid into the driver's seat and turned on the engine. She blinked back tears as she guided the car along the long oak-lined driveway towards the imposing gates to the compound.

3

The Final Kiss

"Mr Humphries?"

"Yes Katie?"

"The Elite is waiting in the gymnasium sir."

"Then I suppose we should proceed."

Mr Humphries looked at his watch. He crossed the large office to a tall-boy and extracted a long, thin cane.

During the weeks that he had spent with Ms Lawton the new Grand Master had familiarized himself with the many traditions of the Back to School unit. Ms Lawton had based the units many rules, regulations, protocols and traditions on its former incarnation as a once respected girl's fee-paying academy.

The Elite was comprised of the twelve inmates serving the last year of their sentences. As the final phase of their social rehabilitation they were given responsibility for overseeing the facility at all times that the inmates were not otherwise engaged in attending tutorials, lectures or other formal curriculum activities.

Members of the Elite were granted thrashing rights over the other inmates and carried short whippy ashplant canes under their arms at all times.

The Ceremonial Thrashing into the Elite fascinated him. Ms Lawton explained that at three o'clock on the first afternoon of each new year the twelve new prefects were assembled in the gymnasium, where prior to receiving their official prefectorial ties, badges and whippy ashplants, they were bent over a vaulting horse and beaten by the Grand Dame.

Ms Lawton told him that the tradition preceded the establishment of the Back to School unit. She informed him that many years earlier she had personally bent over the vaulting horse to be ceremonially thrashed into the Elite and had accepted the beating without question or complaint.

Theoretically it was the last caning an inmate would expect to receive, amongst the Woody Wags the twelfth stroke was known as 'The Final Kiss'.

However, Ms Lawton pointed out that this was not always the case. She recalled her own schooldays. Despite her reputation as the school's naughtiest girl she had been surprisingly appointed the prestigious position of Red-shirt, the most senior member of the Elite. During her tenure she had established a record for being the most caned prefect in the school's history; a record she ironically took over from none other than Patty Hodge.

Prior to the imposition of the austere regime code-named Operation Scorched Arse caning of members of the Elite had been relatively infrequent. However, during Ms Lawton's final year as Grand Dame the whop-rate amongst the Elite had escalated.

Mr Humphries strode into the gymnasium with Katie Beck in his wake. Along the right hand wall of the gym the Brass were seated on lawn chairs. Standing in a line along the opposite wall were twelve of the inmates. They were dressed in crisp white blouses with red braid around the collars and short pleated skirts. The collars of their blouses were unfastened and they were not wearing ties.

A suede-saddled vaulting horse had been placed in the center of the gymnasium floor. The new Grand Master removed his black suit-jacket and handed it to Katie Beck. Methodically he turned back the sleeves of his white shirt to just below the elbow.

Katie Beck handed the Grand Master the long, thin cane he had brought from his office. He flexed it between his hands and then swished it through the air several times. He nodded at Katie.

Katie looked down at her clipboard.

"Brompton," she read, "Lady Victoria."

The Grand Master watched as Lady Victoria Brompton left the line of inmates and strode purposefully towards the vaulting horse. Over the past two days he had spent considerable time with the newly appointed Red-shirt. Victoria had been the only person aside from Mr Humphries, Ms Lawton and members of the Ministry who had known of the Grand Dame's exit strategy and had been sworn to silence. He had observed her poise and self-assurance. She had not demonstrated any signs of the fiery temper or pugnaciousness that Ms Lawton had forewarned him of.

Without any instruction the aristocrat confidently folded herself over the vaulting horse with her backside sitting up proud.

4

Thrashed into the Elite

If Mr Humphries was aware that he had the rapt attention of everybody in the room he didn't show it. He was calm and composed as he stepped forward and neatly folded back Victoria's skirt. She raised her hips cooperatively to allow him to slip her navy blue bumbags down behind her knees and then settled back over the horse, prostrate and acquiescent. The Grand Master raised the cane.

The Grand Master took the stack of items from Katie Beck and handed them to Lady Victoria.

"Well taken, Victoria," he said approvingly, "you may go and change now."

Lady Vix took the pile of clothing, badges and a wood backed hairbrush from Mr Humphries.

"Thank you, sir," she said in an even voice.

The Grand Master was genuinely impressed. He was confident that he had applied the cane with more than enough zip to heat up her rear end considerably. Once or twice she had ridden up on tiptoes, her bottom squirming, but she had immediately returned into position and not a murmur had passed her lips. When it was over and she approached him her face was a little wan but she was dry-eyed and had met his gaze evenly.

He watched her walking back down the gymnasium towards the changing rooms; apart from a certain stiffness to her gait it was impossible to tell that she had just received twelve strokes of the cane across her bare bottom.

Mr Humphries turned to Katie.

"Cox," she said. "Rachel Cox."

Prefect by prefect the Grand Master worked his way down the line, giving them each the 'final kiss', then handing them their blazers, badges and ties of office, and the short whippy ashplants with which they would impose their authority. Rachel, the Deputy Red-shirt, was followed by the most senior prefects. Claire Brooks would be the Dorm Raider, responsible for ensuring that the facility settled down at night. Amanda San Pierre had been selected as the Senior Brat Draper. The two Sally's, Poffley and Cobb, were to act as Captains of the Blue and Red Houses respectively. The six remaining prefects would act in a variety of lesser, but nonetheless important, supporting roles.

The gals took their thrashings with varying degrees of stoicism. Rachel, Claire and Mandy were the bravest, taking their licks without flinching. Before coming down to the gymnasium he had looked over the prefects' records on the Bottoms Up Table of Troublemakers database, known amongst the inmates as the Big BUTT. Of the twelve new members of the Elite only Lady Victoria and Claire had ever received twelve strokes before. Rachel and Amanda had both received nine on several occasions each. The rest of the prefects had maxed out at six so it was not surprising that towards the ends of the thrashings they were beginning to moan and groan and wriggle in agitation. Nonetheless only one of the new Elite made a complete muff of herself.

Helen James was sobbing before she bent over the horse and she howled from the off. She did her best to get up from the horse every time the cane landed but fortunately she was bent too far over to be successful. Mr Humphries waited patiently between strokes while her expansive behind stopped wiggling and jiggling like a jelly that hadn't quite set. Her howls filled the gymnasium and he suspected that they could probably be heard all over the facility. She was openly blubbing when he finally helped her to her feet.

One by one the gals returned from the changing rooms looking spick and span in their new outfits. Lady Victoria Brompton had changed her blouse and was now wearing the red shirt with black braid that signified her official position as the most senior inmate at the facility. Her black tie had the unit's emblem embroidered into it and she wore a metallic badge on the lapel of her blazer with 'Head Gal' on it. The other gals had swapped their striped ties for solid red and they wore block red blazers to segregate them from the rest of the inmates. Under their arms the prefects had tucked the whippy ashplants that they would carry everywhere they went for the remainder of the year.

One by one the prefects stepped forward and recited the Elite pledge. Predictably Helen James's performance was rather lack luster and somewhat marred by the tears still streaming down her face and her strangled sobs a she muttered the words. Mr Humphries shook hands with each prefect and wished them luck. Looking somewhat rueful the prefects wriggled out of the gymnasium, charged with maintaining order at the rambunctious Back to School unit.

A Fine Repast

At six o'clock the inmates received word that they were to repair to the Great Hall to meet with the Grand Master.

Upon their arrival they were startled to find that the hall had been decorated with tables covered in white linen table-clothes, table settings of bone china and expensive silverware and crystal wine glasses.

Earlier in the day Mr Humphries had summonsed Dotty Hammell, the Dame in charge of Domestic Science, and Cassandra Cassidy, to his office.

Prior to being found guilty of Extreme Ladetting Cassandra had owned an exclusive restaurant called Cassie Cassy's.

Mr Humphries had studied the menu of the usual fare on offer to the inmates and had been deeply unimpressed. He saw no reason why the residents of the facility should be subjected to a diet of porridge and gruel shipped in by outside contractors. He drew up a shopping list and instructed Dotty and Cassie to go into town.

To the further surprise of the inmates the Brass had been excluded from the guest list for dinner. Mr Humphries seemed sublimely indifferent to being the sole male amongst a gathering of eighty-four females.

"Tonight is a new beginning," he told them. "I have appointed Cassandra Cassidy as the new head chef of the facility and have given her a generous budget to ensure that the quality of food available is considerably improved. Over the next few weeks we will be outfitting new kitchens and will become self-sufficient. I will establish a rotational kitchen roster and everybody in this room will participate in the preparation of the meals that we share."

The inmates were astonished. A superb tomato and corn soup with fresh basil was followed by crab cakes with avocado garnish. To finish they were served a raspberry trifle with nectarine sauce. To their even greater amazement on each of the tables the Grand Master had provided several bottles of a 2000 Gary Farrell Rochioli-Allen Pinot Noir from the Russian River Valley vineyard that delightfully offered a combination of tart-cherry, lavender, minerals and spices.

In Ms Lawton's day alcohol had been strictly prohibited. Anybody found with booze was publicly flogged in front of the other inmates. An inmate named Bernadette Summers ran an underground operation supplying illicit hooch and other prohibited supplies. She was occasionally caught and flogged but she didn't care, profits were good.

"They can't hurt me," she liked to brag. "I'm the fucking Bounder."

Mr Humphries sat at a table with the members of the red-bottomed Elite. Between courses he circulated the hall introducing himself to each of the inmates and advising them of the timing he had established for their personal performance reviews.

By the time dinner was over the inmates of the Woody Back to School unit were totally bewildered. They had chowed down on their grub appreciatively and had emptied the bottles of wine with relish. Nonetheless, despite their enjoyment of the delightful gastronomic treat they were still vaguely suspicious that this might be some kind of elaborate hoax. After all twelve months earlier their first days back at the facility had a far less appetizing flavor with the implementation of Operation Scorched Arse.

Over the years Ms Lawton had become increasingly concerned with the seemingly unstoppable rise in mega-minxdom. She constantly wrestled with balancing judicious discipline with counter-acting the increasingly powerful cult following of Cathryn Cassidy. Every year the Extreme Ladettes banished to the 'Big House', as the Woody Back to School unit was known, were more rebellious and disciplinary challenged.

With public outcry over Ladette behavior at its peak the Dark Agents of the System were intent on making examples of the so-called Celebrity Ladettes, a group of wealthy and famous playgirls with a reputation for extreme partying. The Celebrity Ladettes were proving amongst the most disciplinary challenged of her charges.

Determined to take a hard-line Ms Lawton had spent the summer months redrafting the rules, regulations and protocols in what became known as the Radical Revisions.

Operation Scorched Arse would start innocuously enough with a minor demeanor by one of the unit's highest-profile and disciplinary challenged Ladettes.

Deborah Morton had been arrested on the center court of Wimbledon having just lost a grueling and exhausting semi-final battle. She was putting her racquets away when the Dark Agents of the System came on court and arrested her. With her hands manacled behind her back she was led from the court in front of millions of TV viewers.

She was charged with Extreme Ladetting and sentenced to seven years at the Big House without the possibility of parole. Deborah Morton quickly became an influential participant in the growing cult of mega-minxdom.

6

Deborah in Disgrace

During each morning assembly the Grand Dame had taken to delivering dire warnings against anybody violating the rules, regulations and protocols.

On Wednesday morning she selected the rules regarding clobber as the subject matter of her address.

The rules, known as 'The Politics of Clobber', amongst the inmates, filled six full pages of the Woody ledger of regulations and referred to another thirty-six detailed protocols. The Grand Dame strongly advised the inmates to reacquaint themselves with the rules and darkly informed them that she had instructed the Brass and the Elite to impose a zero-tolerance policy regarding clobber abuse.

The following morning the inmates were given an ominous insight into Ms Lawton's zero-tolerance imposition of the protocols. The assembled gals had just taken their seats and were waiting for Ms Lawton to launch into her daily diatribe, when to their surprise she stepped towards the front of the stage with a withering look on her face, gazing over the top of her glasses and pointing her finger towards the back of the hall.

"Morton, stand up this instant!" the Grand Dame had roared from the stage.

With a look of total surprise on her face Deborah slowly rose to her feet.

"Your tie is undone, young lady!" The Grand Dame accused in a blistering tone, her finger jabbing the air in the direction of the nonplussed inmate.

Debs hand had involuntarily gone to her neck and she had felt herself redden as every gal in the hall had turned and looked towards the back of the room.

"It was only yesterday that I warned this assembly that I would take not tolerate any further instances of clobber abuse," the Grand Dame fumed. "Nevertheless you have flagrantly chosen to ignore my warning and turn up for assembly in this most disgraceful and unkempt manner." She reached into her jacket pocket and produced a red card. "I think you had better go and wait outside my study so we can discuss this matter further."

Deborah looked taken aback and hesitated momentarily. Once again the Grand Dame raised her voice angrily. "Leave the hall this instant young lady," she barked from the stage. "Unless you would prefer for me to have you removed?"

Crimson faced, Deborah was forced to struggle passed her seated chums, before making her way through the hall with every eye fixed upon her. Her fellow inmates were gaping in bewilderment.

Upon her return to the facility Deborah had entered Phase Five of her sentence and was now considered to be a senior inmate. Traditionally seniors had always been afforded a number of courtesies that they had not enjoyed during the earlier phases of their incarceration. One of the more popular concessions was that in the event the more senior inmates required disciplining they should be treated discretely. The protocols recommended that the offender be taken to one side and be informed privately that they were required to visit the Grand Dame for punishment. The public berating of a Phase Five inmate was a clear departure from protocol and to chuck Deborah out of the assembly hall was unprecedented.

Deborah hurried red-faced down the center aisle, averting her eyes from the inmates. Although she was acutely aware that having her top button unfastened and her tie loosened contravened a zero-tolerance abuse of clobber protocol and attracted a mandatory caning, she was bewildered as to why the Grand Dame would have chosen to embarrass her in such a public manner. Despite her high ranking on the Hall of Shame, Deborah Morton was considered to be the unit's golden gal. She was the facility's top student, regularly played clarinet as a guest with local orchestras and despite her suspension from professional tennis she still won many prestigious amateur tournaments. Her achievements had brought significant kudos to the reputation and public perception of the success of the Woody Back to School experiment. She strode passed the stage with her head slightly bowed, not wanting to look up at the Grand Dame.

Glowering, Deborah pushed the doors of the assembly hall open and stomped into the corridor.

She cut along sharpish knowing that the Grand Dame wouldn't continue with assembly until the sound of her footsteps could no longer be heard inside the hall.

7

Deborah in Denial

The hall was silent bar the sound of Deborah's retreating footsteps. Ms Lawton pushed her glasses back up her nose and rearranged her papers while she waited to commence assembly. She cleared her throat and looked up over the assembled inmates. To her surprise she saw Yvonne Godfrey standing up, waving a red card in her right hand.

"What is it Godfrey?" she asked impatiently.

"It's Cassidy Ma'am," Godders said gleefully and touched her left index finger to the knot of her own tie.

During assembly it was Yvonne's task to stand at the end of the row that the Phase Two inmates frequented and monitor them for gabbing, goofing, larking or pranking.

The Grand Dame scanned the row of inmates until she spotted Cassandra Cassidy seated halfway along. Janet was quite correct; Cassie Cassy's tie was equally delinquent as Deborah's.

"Alright Cassidy," the Grand Dame said tightly, "Get out. Go and get yourself inspected."

Deborah had nearly reached the end of the corridor when she heard the hall doors swing open and shut again. She turned around and saw Cassandra Cassidy come out of the hall, her tie loosened and a hint of a grin on her face.

Debs waited for Cassie to approach.

"You too?" she asked.

Cassie Cassy nodded. "She's pretty shirty so I guess we're in for some good, tight whops."

"Hmmph!" grunted Deborah sullenly.

As they made their way through the labyrinth of corridors that led to the Grand Dames study Cassie tried to make idle conversation but Deborah was unresponsive. She was fond of Cassie Cassy but she was lost in her own disgruntled train of thought.

Debs had been genuinely surprised when the Grand Dame had pointed out her delinquent neckwear. Despite Ms Lawton's accusations it had been a genuine oversight. Each morning Deborah rose an hour early for tennis practice with her coach, Ms Lummell. After they had finished practicing serves, lobs and slices Deborah generally completed her training by running several laps around the compound. That morning she had been feeling quite active and had added an extra lap. The additional time had meant that she had had to rush into the shower and then finish dressing as she dashed through the quadrangle to the assembly hall. She had merely forgotten to finish by fastening her collar and tightening her tie.

The more Debs thought about it the more unreasonable her ignominious dismissal from the hall appeared. Although six of the best first thing in the morning was never pleasant, it wasn't the prospect of being caned that incensed Deborah. She ruefully acknowledged that the oversight was foolish, particularly in light of the previous morning's diatribe. If she had been privately taken to one side and sent up she would have accepted her punishment without complaint. Deborah had an unfortunate history of failing to button up properly and held the record for being caned for the same clobber transgression of collar and tie abuse. However, the Grand Dame's decision to publicly disgrace her made her blood boil.

"I'm not going to be whopped for this," Deborah finally muttered as they entered the corridor that lead to the stairwell up to the Grand Dames office.

"Yeah, rock on, Debs," laughed Cassie. "Zero-tolerance collar and tie abuse and you're not going to be whopped?"

Debs shook her head firmly. "This is completely out with the protocols. She had no right to red card me."

Cassie cast Deborah a sideways glance. She didn't like to argue with a more experienced inmate but as far as she knew Ms Lawton was not in the habit of cutting inmates slack on minor technicalities. Cassie knew from experience that collar and tie abuse was one of Ms Lawton's pet peeves and when she said zero-tolerance she meant it. It occurred to Cassie Cassy that Debs might be laboring in an unhealthy state of denial. Nonetheless, she nodded at Deborah and assured her everything would straighten itself out.

When the two gals arrived at the landing outside the Grand Dame's study the door to Katie Beck's office was wide open. Cassandra Cassidy crossed the landing and went in.

"I need to be inspected," she muttered.

8

Inspection

Katie Beck had finished her sentence as an inmate of the Woody Back to School unit several years earlier and had left the facility to attend college under the graduation program available to inmates who had been successfully socially rehabilitated.

However, Katie hated being away from the unit, where she had acted as the all-powerful Red-shirt. Several years earlier while she was still incarcerated her parents had died tragically in a car accident. Generously Ms Lawton had formally adopted her to avoid a Court Appointed Guardian being appointed by the Dark Agents of the System. Katie had prevailed upon her guardian to allow her to return as a member of staff. Finally Ms Lawton had agreed and appointed her adopted daughter as an administrative assistant. Katie had been dissatisfied with her lowly status and had persuaded the Grand Dame to give her an official title of Matron and quickly wormed her way into a position as the Beak's unofficial aide de camp.

The return of Katie had been unpopular with the inmates. Her spell as Red-shirt had been particularly tyrannical. She had sworn to beat the backside of every inmate during her first hundred days of office and had accomplished her target in half the time. As Matron, Katie had conspired to continue from where she had left off as Red-shirt. She persuaded Ms Lawton to extend the rules and protocols of the Politics of Clobber and worked covertly with Patty Hodge to promote a resurgence of the Secret Sorority of Serial Spankers within the Elite. As her heinous power and influence grew she convinced the Grand Dame to allow her to implement a system of bottom inspection for gals about to get six from the Beak. Theoretically it was to ensure that a gal's backside was in a suitable state to accommodate six strokes of the senior cane from the Grand Dame. However, Katie chose to use bottom inspection as a time to add further hurt and humiliation to the luckless victim.

The unfortunate recipient of the impending caning was forced to go into the ante-room adjoining Katie's office, lower her bumbags, flip up her skirt and spread-eagle herself chest down across a large wooden desk. In her own sweet time Katie would come in and carry out her inspection, which would generally involve pinching, prodding and poking before she decreed the gal to be in a perfect state for six of the best.

After a few minutes Cassie Cassy reappeared on the landing and without provocation turned to face the wall, placing her hands on her head and pressing her nose against the wood paneling.

"Well, what are you waiting for Morton?" Katie called expectantly.

"I'm waiting for the Beak," growled Deborah.

"Get your arse in here for inspection," said Katie impatiently.

"I don't need to be inspected," said Deborah defiantly, "I ain't here for a licking."

By the time they had reached the landing Deborah had convinced herself that when the Grand Dame arrived she would have calmed down and would accept Deb's explanation regarding her delinquent neckwear. She was also certain that the Grand Dame would acknowledge that her departure from protocol was punishment enough and would let the matter drop.

Katie stepped out onto the landing. She peered at Deborah. "What do you mean you're not here for a licking?" she demanded. "You were booted out of assembly weren't you?"

Deborah glared at Katie. "It was just a spur of the moment thing; the Beak got shirty and wasn't thinking straight. It'll all be sorted when she gets here."

"Are you refusing to be inspected?" gasped Katie incredulously.

"I'm telling you I'm not here to be licked," said Deborah emphatically, "so there ain't any inspection to refuse."

"I'm going to give you one last chance Morton," hissed Katie, "now get in my office and bend over the desk."

"I ain't being inspected," retorted Debs categorically. "You gonna try and make me."

Katie looked uncertain; in the past three years she had been required to inspect hundreds of gals, including Deborah on sundry occasions, and she had never once been refused. Katie didn't share Deborah's opinion that she wasn't about to be whopped but Debs was extremely physically fit and although she was shorter than Katie, the Matron didn't fancy her chances at physically forcing the athlete to bend over the desk. Katie Beck decided the better part of valor was to await the arrival of Ms Lawton.

"You'd better do nose and toes," said Katie.

"Fuck nose and toes," muttered Deborah.

"What did you say?" snapped Katie.

"Nothing," grunted Debs.

Cassie Cassy giggled.

"And you can keep quiet Cassidy," the Matron snapped at Cassie, "else you'll be over my knee before you know it."

Katie Beck shot a hostile glance at Debs, and then she retreated back into her office.

Deborah leaned back against the wall, crooking her knee and stuffing her hands in the pockets of her red and black striped blazer.

9

Defiant Debs

It was a full twenty minutes before the two gals heard the sound of the Grand Dame's high heels click clacking as she approached along the corridor below.

As Deborah had predicted Ms Lawton's mood had mellowed somewhat since her spontaneous outburst in the hall. The Grand Dame had been astonished to see Debs slouching in her seat at the back of the hall with the collar of her blouse open and her tie hanging loose. Under normal circumstances she would have been irritated and would have made a mental note to tell the new Red-shirt, Penelope Ann Evans, to discretely send the Debs up for a bare bender once assembly was finished. However, Deborah's apparent display of brazen defiance of the previous morning's warning sent the Grand Dame into a fit of apoplexy.

Nonetheless, she was fond of Deborah and recognized that she had probably been a little harsh in humiliating her by publicly chucking her out of the hall. Clearly, according to protocol, Deborah deserved to be caned but Ms Lawton knew she could have handled the matter with a little more delicacy. As she turned into the stairwell she was beginning to vie towards a compromise.

Ms Lawton's feeling of détente was instantly reversed when she stepped onto the landing. Her mouth opened disbelievingly as she stared at Deborah. Debs was leaning back against the wall with her hands stuffed in the pockets of her blazer and a recalcitrant pout on her face.

"Why aren't you facing the wall Morton?" the Grand Dame spluttered incredulously.

Deborah glared at the Grand Dame darkly. Slowly she took her hands from the pockets of her blazer and let them fall to her sides. She moved away from the wall and pulled her shoulders back.

"I'm sorry Ma'am, I didn't think it was necessary," she mumbled, but there was no sign of apology on her sullen face.

"Not necessary? What the devil are you talking about, not necessary?" Ms Lawton asked sharply. She scowled at Deborah. "And wipe that ugly pout off your face this instant."

Deborah seethed inwardly. It was obvious that the Grand Dame was still very cross but she didn't see any need for her to be so abrupt.

She glared back at the Grand Dame. "You just said you wanted to discuss the matter. Besides, it was just an oversight Ma'am. I stayed to do an extra lap after tennis practice and I had to get dressed in a hurry. I'm sorry, it was just a silly mistake," she said in an overtly recalcitrant tone of voice.

The Grand Dame continued to glower at Deborah Morton. Debs bravado began to wilt a little.

"May I go now?" she asked hopefully.

"You most certainly cannot go, Morton!" the Grand Dame snapped.

At that moment Katie Beck chose to poke her head out of her office.

"Excuse me Grand Dame," she said smugly. "May I have a word? It's about Morton Ma'am, she refused to be inspected."

Deborah glared daggers at Katie. "I did not," she said defiantly, "I've explained that I didn't think it was necessary."

Ms Lawton swung open the door to her office. "I think we'd better go inside Morton, and you can come too Cassidy."

Reluctantly Deborah Morton turned and faced the wall in the Grand Dame's office; she placed her hands on her head and pressed her nose to the wood paneling.

Behind her Cassie Cassy was being scolded. Deborah listened morosely to the Grand Dame's barbed remarks, knowing that Cassie Cassy would be standing in the center of the room having to listen unflinchingly while the Grand Dame worked her over a little before she caned her.

Cassie Cassy removed her blazer and hung it over the back of the straight-backed chair that stood before the fireplace. She bent forward at the waist and reached down until she was gripping the crossbar below the cushioned seat. She felt the pleated skirt of her gymslip being folded back and pushed her hips away from the chair to allow Ms Lawton to roll her navy blue gossamer bumbags down to the tops of her thighs.

Deborah listened as the cane cut through the air, making crisp, emphatic thwacks as it landed across Cassie's unprotected derriere. She continued to seethe inwardly and became increasingly determined to straighten this matter out once and for all.

Ms Lawton's ire at Deborah's show of belligerence had not boded well for Cassie Cassy. The Grand Dame had delivered an extremely tight licking. The first five strokes had produced hot, sweaty tramlines neatly spaced across the crown of the upturned rump and then Ms Lawton had delivered her final stroke diagonally across the stripes. It was a signature Lawton licking, a perfect five-bar gate.

10

A Spanking for Debs Morton

Deborah Morton stood before the Grand Dame, her body resting into an insolent slouch. Ms Lawton's face was a picture of exasperation. She took Deborah by the shoulders and shook her.

"Stop slouching," she snapped, "and stand up straight."

Deborah shrugged herself free of the Grand Dame and slowly stood to attention.

"What the devil has got into you Morton?" the Grand Dame asked coldly. "I have never seen such petulant behavior. Do you think I issue orders for them to be simply ignored?"

"No, Ma'am, of course not."

"Yet you chose to flagrantly ignore my instructions?"

"It was just a silly mistake. I told you that I'd just come from tennis practice and I changed in a hurry. I really don't understand what all the fuss is about," Deborah said hotly.

"Yes it was silly Morton. Very silly indeed," the Grand Dame responded slowly, "but your attitude is even sillier. You will receive six strokes of the cane for zero-tolerance clobber abuse and a further six strokes for gross belligerence."

"A double bender for having my tie undone?" Deborah interjected contemptuously. "Don't be bloody ridiculous. I'm a senior...!" Deborah couldn't help herself. It was unthinkable. Debs' mind was racing. She wasn't having this.

"If you interrupt me again young lady I'll..."

"You'll what? Spank me?" Deborah snapped back petulantly.

The next thing Deborah Morton knew she was being spun around and pinned down, chest forward, across the top of the desk.

The Grand Dame thumped her hand down on the seat of Deborah's skirt. Debs struggled and squirmed and tried to get free.

"Lemme go!" she squealed. She kicked back with her left leg and caught Ms Lawton painfully below the knee. The Grand Dame grunted with displeasure.

"Right that does it," she growled. She yanked Debs up from the desktop, grabbed her by the wrist and marched her across the room. It all happened so fast that Debs had no time to resist. In a matter of seconds Ms Lawton had sunk down onto a sofa and Debs found herself tumbling helplessly downwards.

The Grand Dame put her hand firmly on the back of Deborah's neck pushing her head down; she flipped back Debs skirt and yanked down her bumbags.

"Heyyyyyyy!!!" wailed Deborah. "What the fuck are you doing?"

Ms Lawton ignored the expletive and responded with a salvo of spanks. Deborah tried to wrestle free but Ms Lawton took a tight grip around her waist and pulled her in tightly to the fold of her lap. The Grand Dame delivered the spanks fast and hard in a fashion known to the Woody Wags as the blitz attack. Deborah had no time to even catch her breath before her bumbags were yanked back up and she was being dragged to her feet.

Deborah Morton gaped at the Grand Dame incredulously. "You spanked me," she spluttered unnecessarily.

"Yes Morton, I spanked you and now I intend to beat you," Ms Lawton said curtly. "Now go next door and get yourself inspected."

Deborah Morton shuffled out of the room in a minor state of shock. Despite Ms Lawton's petite appearance she had hands like house-bricks and Deborah's bottom was burning furiously. She squirmed across the landing and went into Katie's office.

"I need to be inspected," she said rather lamely.

Katie Beck chuckled. "So you're not here for a licking?" she chortled sarcastically. "Well get yourself in the ante-room and bend over the desk."

Deborah reached under her skirt and rolled down her bumbags. She hitched up the back of her skirt and tucked it into her red waist sash. Despondently she slithered her upper torso across the wooden desktop.

Katie cackled as she ran her fingers over the glowing orbs.

"Oh my," she observed, "that stick is really going to smart. She just had a new consignment delivered. I hear that this year's collection is very whippy."

Deborah contemplated the wisdom of hacking Katie Beck in the shins, but in her first rational decision of the day she sensibly erred on the side of caution. She rearranged her bumbags and smoothed down her skirt. She shot Katie a hostile glare and stomped out of the room.

As she entered the landing Cassie Cassy came out of the Grand Dames study. "Good luck," she whispered and wriggled into the stairwell.

Debs took a deep breath and turned the doorknob.

11

A Double Bare Bender

Deborah bent over the chair unenthusiastically. She was bitterly disappointed at Ms Lawton's harsh behavior. A double bare bender was unheard of except for the rare occasions a member of the Elite needed beating. Deborah felt the cane tap down and squeezed her eyes tightly shut.

Despite her show of belligerence and bravado once she was doubled over the back of the straight-backed chair Deborah was becomingly increasingly anxious. The prospect of a twelve stroke bare bender, delivered over a well-spanked arse, was not in the least bit appealing.

Ms Lawton took a tight grip on the cane. It was exactly the type of overt willfulness that Deborah had displayed that she was determined to stamp out with her radical revisions to the rules, regulations and protocols.

With a new influx of disciplinary challenged inmates she considered it prudent to demonstrate that she meant business immediately.

Ms Lawton knew that even if Cassie Cassy kept quiet, she could rely on Katie Beck to initiate rumors on the Woody gossvine that not only had Debs received a double bare bender, but even worse she had been unceremoniously dragged over the Grand Dame's lap and had her bottom smacked.

Ms Lawton was convinced that making such a high-profile example of a member of the notorious Famous Four would send a resounding message to the inmates and prove to be a major coup in her strategy to counter minxdom.

The Grand Dame raised the cane in the air and brought her arm down swiping.

Deborah gritted her teeth as the cane slashed across her naked, swollen flesh. The most she had ever previously received had been nine strokes and she had considered that very tough duty indeed. She squeezed her eyes shut as the heat of each stripe seemed to attack the core of her central nervous system and sent electric shocks from her head to her toes. However, she was determined to maintain position and refrain from giving the Grand Dame any indication of the distress she was going through. Deborah Morton was not about to make a muff of herself.

Deborah Morton was furious. She was lying face down across her best chum Rosemary Booker's lap having her bottom soothed with a selection of Rosie's mystical potions.

"How dare she?" Deborah ranted. "She's fucking barking! The woman's lost her marbles. She fucking spanked me in front of Cassie!"

"Cassie hasn't said a word," Jojo reassured her.

Deborah grunted. "Yeah, well Katie saw my arse up close and personal. It'll be all over the gossvine by now," she fumed.

Rosemary massaged a new prototype aloe-vera cream into her best chums smoldering rear end. "Well she was certainly on form," she said sympathetically, "these stripes are in terribly tight formation."

Joanna Heyworth and Nicola Jane Nixon were inspecting the cane damage with seasoned eyes.

"A double bare bender and every one landed in the target zone. There's not a single wraparound," said Nixdown admiringly. "That was a very professional job."

"Can't avoid some over-lapping in a double bender," agreed Jojo, "but that's about as safe as it gets."

"If you've quite finished discussing my poor beleaguered bum," grumbled Deborah, "we've got work to do!"

Deborah refused to acknowledge that her belligerence had been ill advised and assured her chums that she was going to get her own back on the Grand Dame.

Deborah's chums were sympathetic but reminded her that it was far from the first time she had been caned for clobber abuse.

"Oh listen to you, the Queen of collar and tie abuse complaining you got another licking," drawled Nixdown.

"That ain't the point," muttered Debs darkly, "she shouldn't have chucked me out of the hall like that. It was a direct contravention of the protocols."

"And you've never been chucked out of assembly before?" laughed Nix cynically.

Her chums cautioned Debs that loudly conspiring to get back at Ms Lawton could have unhealthy ramifications for a gal's bumbags, but Deborah refused to listen.

Even if the Grand Dame was within her rights to cane her, Deborah argued, she had no business screaming at her and chucking her out of the hall like that, and even less business spanking her in front of Cassie Cassy as if she was some recalcitrant grubby. Protocols were established and Ms Lawton had clearly breached them. Debs was determined to get even.

She pouted and sulked when her three chums politely declined her invitation to participate in Debs' revenge.

12

The Radical Revisions

The Grand Dame's demeanor was not greatly improved when Joanna Heyworth and Nicola Jane Nixon were required to pay her a visit the following morning. Ms Lawton stared across her desk and fixed Jojo and Nix with a gimlet glare. She was not in the least bit impressed by their woefully insincere looks of penitence.

Neither gal had offered much in the way of an explanation, merely informing the Principal that Ms Reed, the Dame in charge of Mathematics, had sent them up for disrupting her lecture. Jojo had added that the Maths Dame had requested that they were to be beaten soundly.

The Grand Dame was considerably vexed to find the two chums appearing before her and went to great pains to articulate her displeasure by serving up a most unsavory ration of tongue pie.

Over the years Ms Lawton had perfected the fine art of scolding; she spoke in a cold and clipped manner, selecting her words carefully and spitting barbs across the desk in a tone that resembled diamond running down glass. Occasionally at unexpected moments she would lean forward and unleash a verbal assault that made her victims recoil as if a tiger had swiped its paw at them. The Woody Wags liked to joke that the Grand Dame sat up at night poring over ancient dictionaries, lexicons, tomes and scrolls researching new definitions of mischief and malfeasance.

On occasions she had been known to reduce the more vulnerable inmates to tears long before she took her cane to their backsides, but the Grand Dame knew that she had a snowballs chance in hell of eliciting such an extreme reaction from the two seasoned miscreants standing before her. Jojo and Nix had long ago learned the art of looking repentant and attentive whilst staring into the middle distance and trying to ignore the scathing diatribes.

The Grand Dame had no shortage of ammunition to fuel her vitriolic. Joanna Heyworth was the unit's undisputed Big BUTT and was widely acknowledged to be the most fabulous mega-minx yet to emerge from the ranks of the Bottoms Up Table of Troublemakers. Her best chum, Nicola Jane Nixon, was no shrinking violet either and was a high ranking member on the Hall of Shame. For the past four years Jojo and Nix had dedicated themselves to the cult of minxdom, honing their skills in japing the Brass and rubbishing the Elite. They were amongst Ms Lawton's most frequent visitors.

Jojo fixed her gaze on the painting on the wall behind the Grand Dame. It was one of her favorites, an early work by a famous French impressionist, filled with subtle detail and dozens of characters attending a bacchanalian picnic on the banks of the Seine. It was an original, on loan to the Woody Back to School unit from the private collection of Joe Summers, the notorious scoundrel and fraudster, and father of Bernadette Summers. Sadly Joe was languishing in chokey doing a fifteen year stretch for ripping the government off for millions in international aid grants. Bernadette had lent the facility the paintings for safe keeping while she completed her own seven year stretch. During her regular visits to the Principal's office Jojo had memorized every square inch of the painting and spent hours in the art-room practicing the techniques of the artist. It was a fruitful way to avoid listening to the endless harangues.

Nonetheless, every now and again Ms Lawton's lecture piqued Jojo's interest and curiosity. Ever since they had returned from furlough, during morning assemblies, the Grand Dame had been issuing dire warnings about the painful consequences of continued contravention of the rules, regulations and protocols. Jojo had heard it all before, but this morning Ms Lawton was constantly referring to undisclosed Radical Revisions that she tended to implement. It occurred to Jojo that Radical Revisions might have ominous ramifications for her already beleaguered bumbags.

Throughout the summer furlough Susan Lawton had labored over her strategy to counteract the surge of mega-minxdom that threatened to reduce the unit into anarchy.

When she had first authored the rules, regulations and protocols that would dominate life at the facility she had made the assumption that the inmates would respond positively to the austere disciplinary regime and would become considerably less disciplinary challenged during the latter years of their incarceration. However the subterranean cult of mega-minxdom continued to flourish and many of its leading lights were in the late stages of their sentences. Cat Cassidy, Melanie White, Lady Victoria Brompton and Claire Brooks were all seniors and still raising Cain on the Hall of Shame. Now, within days of commencing the fifth phase of their sentences three members of the notorious Famous Four had already required punishment.

The time had come, the Grand Dame decided, to implement the Radical Revisions before anarchy prevailed.

13

A World Class Whopping

The Grand Dame uttered more dark warnings about her intentions to restore order and to stamp out the cult of mega-minxdom once and for all.

Jojo and Nixdown watched as Ms Lawton strode across the room to the tallboy where she kept her wide selection of canes. The Grand Dame was an elegant woman who was always neatly coifed and immaculately made-up. She always wore stylish suits, with knee length skirts and tailored jackets.

Ms Lawton tested several canes by flexing them and swishing them through the air before settling on one that satisfied her.

She turned away from the cupboard and pointed the cane at Nicola Jane.

"You, Nixon," she snapped, "face the wall."

Sullenly Nicola Jane Nixon walked across the room, knowing exactly what was expected of her. She stepped up to the wood paneled wall and moved in close. She leaned her neck slightly forward until the tip of her nose was gently touching the wall. She shuffled her shoes against the skirting board. She raised her arms and inter-linked her fingers on top of her head.

Nose and toes was a familiar pose to the Woody gals.

The Grand Dame turned and pointed the cane towards Jojo. "You, Heyworth," she snapped, "remove your blazer and bend over the chair."

The eight words had an air of finality about them. Any last bastion of hope of reprieve or forgiveness was immediately vanquished by the simple phrase.

Jojo took her time. She bent forward over the back of the chair and placed her hands on the cushioned seat. She looked down at the familiar faded green covering of the chair seat, then wearily she leaned over further and grasped the cross bar. Once she was in position the Grand Dame stepped forward and turned back the hem of her skirt in neat folds. She felt a tug on the tails of her blouse and then that was turned back too. Jojo raised her hips slightly away from the chair to allow Ms Lawton to roll her bumbags down to the tops of her thighs.

Jojo took a deep breath and tried to settle in. She felt the cane tap down, once, twice, thrice as the Grand Dame got her measure, then from above she heard an ominous whistle, followed by a loud thwack as the cane collided with her upturned behind.

Jojo blinked as the sharp stripe imploded through her central nervous system.

"Its only whops, its only whops," she repeated over and over in her head.

The canes that Ms Lawton favored were hand-crafted from premium grade rattan. They were steamed and stretched before being saturated with a linseed oil compound for several weeks, then finally dried and varnished. The Grand Dame purchased her canes from the same workshop that had supplied the original Woody School and Susan Lawton could personally attest to the superior sting and smart that the thirty-six inch long canes could impart.

Jojo gritted her teeth as the cane sliced across her upturned buttocks. There was no question that the Beak was laying it on thick. The second stroke had landed millimeters below the first with the accuracy of a heat seeking missile, landing perfectly in the target area known as the sweet spot to the Woody Wags.

Despite her acute irritation Ms Lawton was a consummate professional. The Grand Dame did not allow her emotions get the better of her; she was determined to administer a good tight licking.

The Grand Dame caned hundreds of backsides every year and knew that precision and accuracy was the key to delivering a world-class whopping. She caned at a leisurely pace, allowing thirty seconds to elapse between strokes.

Jojo settled in to the rhythm of the caning, repeating her mantra over and over in her head and concentrating on staying in the zone. No matter how hard she was being whopped Jojo understood the importance of putting it up and keep it up. And, no matter how much it hurt she would never make a muff of herself by howling or blubbing.

Jojo's rise to the pinnacle of the Hall of Shame had been truly spectacular. She had dedicated herself to a lifestyle of goofing, larking, japing and pranking and had displaced Woody legends like April Turner, Cat, Melons, Lady Vix and Claire Brooks as the undisputed All-Time Big BUTT. During the fourth year of her sentence Jojo Heyworth had crowned her achievements by becoming the first inmate to be punished fifty times in a single year, scoring what was known to the Woody Wags as 'the Bull'. Miss Jojo Heyworth was more than ready and able to endure a world class whopping and keep on bopping.

14

Miss Jojo Heyworth

When Jojo had first entered the facility she had been sporting a virgin arse. The school that she had attended had not practiced any form of physical discipline and the home she was raised in was a spank-free zone.

However, Jojo had not been altogether unfamiliar with the subject of corporal punishment. She was long-term chums with Nicola Jane Nixon and Claire Brooks. They had ridden together on numerous trophy winning equestrian teams and at the time of their sentencing they were all hotly tipped to star on the next Olympic team.

Nicola Jane and Claire had both attended boarding schools where corporal punishment was prevalent and often regaled Jojo with tales of their misdeeds and the painful consequences. On several occasions her team-mates had turned up for gymkhanas sporting angry weals across their backsides. It had occurred to Jojo that sporting a well-striped arse would probably make competitive horse-back riding a tad uncomfortable.

After leaving school, Jojo Heyworth and Nicola Jane Nixon had teamed up to establish a successful multi-media company. Jojo had produced a number of acclaimed alternative theatrical productions and her murals and sculptures had been shown at several West End Galleries. Nicola Jane, was the daughter of an internationally renowned film producer, and had followed in her father's footsteps and begun to make a niche for herself shooting risqué videos for some of the hottest music acts in town. Many of the videos had featured Nicola Jane in a variety of spanking poses, including her being caned in her old school uniform.

Jojo had found her business partner's predilections slightly curious. Nix had always been extremely vocal about her dislike of being caned at the various schools she had attended. She had been expelled from several for retaliating at being caned by hacking the Headmistresses in the shins. Ultimately she had ended up in reform school after she had fire-bombed the Headmistress' car after being caned in front of her assembled school-mates. Nonetheless, Jojo rarely passed comment. After all Nicola Jane had always been a tad quirky and the videos sold like hot cakes.

Jojo and Nixdown were making out like bandits and the two chums quickly became the toast of the West End party circuit.

Unfortunately the height of their success coincided with another period of fiscal imprudence by the government. Faced with considerable criticism from the Great Unwashed the mandarins of spin were instructed to create a diversion. Bounties on the bumbags of Celebrity Ladettes were increased substantially.

Successful and entrepreneurial young females like Jojo and Nix made ideal targets for the Dark Agents of the System. The Celebrity Goon Squad monitored their every move and covertly photographed them as they left the hottest night-clubs in the Smoke.

Jojo and Nix were arrested on several occasions and hauled before disciplinary tribunals. They were charged with Misdemeanor Ladetting but even the System was forced to acknowledge that the evidence was fragile at best and they were released. However, the Dark Agents were not about to let a pair of substantial bounties go to waste and used their contacts in the conservative press to launch a series of scurrilous attacks on Jojo and Nix.

The blood-thirsty hacks from the right-wing rags denounced the two chums as degenerates and criticized their high-profile life-styles for influencing and encouraging the perpetuation of the Ladette movement. The accusations were ridiculous but the Great Unwashed is a fickle bunch and immediately demanded action.

Jojo and Nix were arrested again and taken to a secret silo of the System. As there were no actual charges to be brought against them the members of the System's disciplinary council sat in-camera. Jojo and Nix were denied legal representation or the opportunity to defend themselves and were found guilty of 'Conspiracy to promote anti-social Ladette behavior amongst the public at large'. They were sentenced to seven years at the Big House without the possibility of parole.

They were taken to a haberdasherers to be measured up. Within twenty-four hours Jojo and Nix found themselves immersed in the Woody world of Whops and Clobber.

15

A Formal Draping

During her induction week at the facility Jojo was assigned a mentor from the Elite who was responsible for indoctrinating her in the labyrinthine of rules, regulations and protocols that would govern her new life. As part of her initiation she was subjected to a number of training spankings from her mentor, or 'Personal Draper,' as she was known. Jojo was taught the correct protocols for arranging herself into the traditional full drape and trained to put it up and keep it up throughout a spanking. She was instilled with the Woody creed that 'only muffs howl'.

At night, after the long days of being mentored, the new inmates were locked up in a Spartan dormitory with twelve beds set up in two rows along the walls with no privacy. Invariably before the lights were turned out and the facility went into lockdown mode they would swap the intimate details of their daily training spankings and hypothesize over their futures in the austere environment that they had been so rudely thrust into.

It did not take long for Jojo to discover just how austere her new environment would prove to be. During the first formal week of term she became the first of the newbie's to be formally draped. A relatively innocuous, but ill-advised, interjection into a geography lecture resulted in her being invited to step up before the form by Ms Wharton.

Jojo's mentor had cautioned her about the Wart. Robin Wharton was a card-carrying member of the Radical Right of the Brass and a notorious tyrant. Jojo couldn't help but notice the wolfish grin of glee on the Dame's face as she sat down on a chair and patted her lap, indicating for her victim to go over and up.

Despite a feeling of trepidation and her slight embarrassment at being upended and turned head down, arse up in front of relative strangers Jojo gritted her teeth and toughed it out.

The Wart spanked Jojo slowly, working up one side of her bumbags and back down the other in series of three's. All the while Ms Wharton kept up a running, and in Jojo's view a wholly unnecessary, commentary.

Once she was finished the Wart post-processed the spanking and made the legendary first entry into the small red-covered Punishment Record Book that Jojo was required to carry at all times in the breast pocket of her blazer. Once this was completed she sent Jojo back to her desk, instructing her to climb up on to the seat of her chair and spend the remainder of the lecture with her hands cradled on top of her head.

Much to her surprise Jojo found herself at the center of attention amongst her new acquaintances and the subject of considerable admiration for her stoic behavior. Miss Joanna Heyworth had been formally inducted into the world of Whops and Clobber.

Life as a Little Brat could be tough. When they were not in the lecture rooms or in the hall completing assignments they were at the permanent disposal of their Personal Drapers. Every minute of free time was taken up with running errands, cleaning the prefect's studies and performing other duties, known as 'grubbing' in Woody parlance.

Nonetheless Jojo found time to study Cathryn Cassidy's subversive doctrine, 'the Manifesto of Mega-minxdom' and was an instant convert. Joanna and Nicola Jane quickly formed a bond with two other celebrity Ladettes, Debs Morton and Rosemary Booker. Like Jojo and Nix, Debs and Rosie had been stitched up like kippers by the Dark Agents of the System in pursuit of the huge bounties paid for diverting the Great Unwashed from the government's numismatic buffoonery.

The four new chums soon began to get themselves spanked with record-breaking frequency. They were highly competitive, matching each other spank for spank and raising the bar for inventive goofing, japing, pranking and larking to an unprecedented standard.

Despite the tradition of alienating the Little Brats during their first year of incarceration and the cynical philosophy that grubbies should be seen and not heard, Jojo, Debs, Nixdown and Rosemary's record-breaking exploits did not go unnoticed by the more seasoned inmates. They soon became known as 'the Famous Four' on the Woody gossvine.

16

The First Brat Beating

The antics of the Famous Four did not pass without comment amongst the Brass. During the spring of Jojo's Brat-year the Radical Right demanded a summit to discuss the 'Problem Brats'. The summit was chaired by Patricia Hodge and the Dame's from the Radical Right sought to persuade Ms Lawton that the hand-spankings were proving ineffectual. They warned the Grand Dame that Brat-minxdom continued to escalate and was in danger of becoming an epidemic.

The fine art of grubbing and the tradition of Brat-draping dates back to the original Woody School and had been introduced by the Lawrence Sisters, who had opened the doors of the academy in 1857. When Ms Lawton had attended the school the system had still been in place and she had first hand experience of the tough life of being a grubby.

When she was commissioned to establish the nation's harshest Back to School unit she was fully cognizant that the inmates were to be comprised of the kingdom's most Extreme Ladette's. It occurred to her that there would be no better antidote to their wild and truculent behavior than to spend their first year as fully paid up grubby's. She hoped that spending twelve months in the somewhat demeaning position of head down, arse up across their Personal Drapers knees might knock some of the recalcitrance out of them.

Ms Lawton was forced to agree that Patty and her cronies had a compelling argument. Even the more minx-friendly Dames from the Liberal Left concurred that the Famous Four were the most disruptive influences that they had yet had to contend with.

The Grand Dame studied the statistics. In sheer volume of spanks Nicola Jane Nixon out-ranked the other members of the Famous Four; however Ms Lawton acknowledged that Nix was at a severe disadvantage. She had been assigned to grub for the presiding Red-shirt, Katie Beck. Katie was proving to be a cruel and autocratic leader of the Elite and Ms Lawton had already been forced to cane her on several occasions for over-stepping the boundaries established in the Red-shirt Charter. The majority of Nixdown's spankings had been delivered by her mentor. Amongst the Famous Four she had been spanked the least for disrupting lectures.

The Grand Dame looked at the second name on the list. She summonsed a grubby.

"Find Heyworth," she instructed. "Tell her I wish to see her and advise her that she had better cut along sharpish."

"Remove your blazer and bend over the chair," Ms Lawton had instructed Jojo. "I intend to give you three strokes of the cane for serial malfeasance." Joanna Heyworth stared at the straight-backed chair that stood ominously in front of the fireplace in the Grand Dame's study.

Uncertainly Joanna had leaned forward, her hands on the padded seat, her legs slightly buckled. The Grand Dame tapped her knees with the cane.

"Straight legs Heyworth, reach down and grasp the cross bar. I need you to put it up and keep it up," she commanded.

Joanna reached downwards, she was keenly conscious that as she reached towards the crossbar her bottom was sticking further and further up in the air. Her heart pounded beneath her blouse as she felt her skirt being turned back.

It was a historic moment: Jojo Heyworth was about to become the first Little Brat in the unit's history to be caned.

The first stroke of the cane swiped across Joanna's bottom. For a second she thought it wasn't so bad and then the wave of agitation enveloped her. She had never experienced anything like it in her life. The electrifying force of the stripe of the thin stick seemed to explore nerve endings she was not even aware existed. Momentarily she felt concussed, then as the mist of sheer pain subsided she had a second of lucidity and thought to herself, "Yikes, I hope there's not many more from where that came from." And then the second stroke landed.

Jojo was sitting uncomfortably in the cafeteria surrounded by Rosemary, Nix and Debs. Predictably they were engrossed in discussing Joanna's recent encounter with the Grand Dame's cane. They were taken by surprise when Lady Victoria Brompton barreled down on their table.

Jojo and her chums had become used to being ignored by the more senior inmates and they were not sure what to make of Victoria's arrival.

Although she was only in the second phase of her sentence Lady Vix was already a Woody legend and was a top lieutenant in Cat Cassidy's subversive cult of mega-minxdom. She had a reputation as a pugnacious, potty-mouthed firebrand.

Vix put both hands on the table and stared directly at Jojo.

"Rumor has it you got whopped, that true?" she asked.

Jojo nodded.

"You howl?" demanded Victoria.

Jojo shook her head.

"You sure?" asked Victoria.

Joanna nodded again. "Jojo doesn't howl," she said emphatically. "Only muffs howl."

Lady Vix held Jojo's stare.

"Fawkin' 'A' sister," she chuckled finally and then turned on her heel and returned to her seat.

17

From Nix to Nixdown

The fifth stroke slashed down causing Jojo to take a sharp intake of breath. She shook her head in an attempt to clear the fog of pain and desperately struggled to prepare herself for the final stroke, known amongst the Woody Wags as 'the Closer'.

Ms Lawton's trademark was the five-bar gate. She would lay out the first five strokes evenly across the crown of her victims bum and then slash the final stroke down diagonally across the earlier stripes.

Jojo winced as the cane sliced down, agitating the thin, swollen stripes that covered her behind. She gripped the chair wrung and closed her eyes. The heat of the stripe passed through her in waves and she concentrated on keeping her breathing even.

Ms Lawton reached down and rolled Joanna's bumbags back in to place and then folded her skirt down.

"You may rise," she said unsympathetically. "Go and face the wall." The Grand Dame pointed at Nicola Jane. "Nixon," she snapped. "Remove your blazer and bend over the chair."

As the two chums crossed over in the middle of the office Jojo threw Nixdown a wry grin. The two gals had made many forays to the Grand Dame's study together. Since they had been sentenced to spend seven years at the Woody Back to School unit they had made the perpetration of maximum mischief and mayhem their raison d'etre.

Nicola Jane Nixon shrugged off her striped blazer and after giving Ms Lawton a belligerent glare she bent over the chair.

Nixdown was a queer duck by any standards. She had a reputation for being rude, deeply cynical and spectacularly promiscuous. When she was able to secure weekend town passes she passed the afternoons having nooky with a famous rock-star and during the week she indulged herself by boffing her way through the Elite.

Nix made no secret of the fact that she despised being formally punished but she adored pain and submission in a recreational theatre. Nixdown had earned her nickname during the unfortunate year when she had been obliged to act as Personal Grubby to Katie Beck. The sadistic Red-shirt had liberally indulged her penchant for sporting spanking and regularly illegally yanked down Nicola Jane's navy blue knickers to deliver unreported drapings. Never one's to miss an opportunity the Woody Wags immediately extended Nicola Jane's lifelong abbreviation from Nix to Nixdown.

A lot of stripes had passed under Nixdown's bumbags since those heady early days of discovering the joys of minxdom. She was a naturally obstreperous cove and her tendency to treat the Brass and the Elite as second class citizens had not proven to be a popular trait. The Brass and Elite branded her a degenerate and laid siege to her bumbags. Her fellow inmates, of course, thought that she was absolutley fabulous.

Standing a mere five feet and half an inch tall in flat soled shoes Nix was forced to raise herself up onto the balls of her feet in order to reach over the chair to grasp the cross bar on the far side.

Nixdown had no time for mantra's she was too busy directing dark hexes at the Grand Dame as her skirt and bumbags were being neatly rearranged. She winced as the cane scorched across her arse. The feverish burn might have sent her into spasms of ecstasy under the right circumstances but bent over the straight-backed chair in Ms Lawton's study it merely caused her to mutter her own version of the motto of the Hellfire Club inscribed on the doorway of Medmenham Abbey. "Fay ce que voudras, Bitch!" Nix muttered under her breath.

Nixdown and Jojo took it in turns to lay across Rosemary's lap so that they could have the hot red stripes on their bottoms anointed with her mystical balms.

"All this gab about Radical Revisions doesn't bode well for our bumbags," predicted Jojo.

"Fuck the Radical Revisions," muttered Nixdown cynically.

"I told you, she's finally lost it," said Debs. "The Beak is certifiably fucking barking."

"Jojo's right, a certifiably barking Beak and a cupboard full of canes do not bode well for our bumbags," observed Rosemary.

18

The Nose and Toes Protocols

On Saturday afternoon Debs Morton was up in the study she shared with Rosemary working on an assignment when there was a knock on the door.

"Excuse me, Morton," said Virginia Gardiner, "but Miss Butcher needs you repair to the library. Apparently you are to be beaten on Red House Business. She said that you need to cut along sharpish."

Deborah scowled darkly at the grubby. Virginia took a wary step backwards. "I'm sorry, Morton," she said hurriedly and beat a hasty retreat.

Dismally Deborah went to the closet and took down her blazer from a clothes-hanger. She pulled it on and fastened the top button before heading out of the door.

The library was housed in the east wing of the sprawling facility and even stretching her legs it took Debs nearly five minutes before she finally entered the corridor leading to the room. As she cut through the labyrinth of hallways and stairwells she wracked her brains as to what she could possibly have done that would merit a beating.

She had started the day with her normal routine of waking at dawn and meeting up with Ms Lummell for a three mile run. They had then taken to the tennis court and worked on her serve for an hour. When they were finished she had changed and attended assembly, which had proved mercifully uneventful. Afterwards she had returned to her study to work on a paper on Thomas a Becket and the Constitutions of Clarenden. Debs was an avid historian and became engrossed in her research; save for a short break in the cafeteria she hadn't left her study.

Debs approached the heavy wooden door at the end of the corridor. Once she reached the entrance to the library she turned to face the wall, leaning slightly forward so that the tip of her nose physically touched the wood panels and then raised her arms and inter-linked her fingers on the top of her head.

Deborah knew the form; it would be a minimum of fifteen minutes before the House Captain would arrive, leaving her an appropriate interval to ruminate over the imminent future of her bumbags. Although the seventy-two hours that had elapsed since her double bare bender from Ms Lawton was adequate time for a whop-hardened veteran like Debs to make a full recovery she was less than enthused by the prospect of embarking on another licking in quite such short proximity.

She stared gloomily at the wall. Somewhere in the distance she could hear the sound of footsteps as they climbed the wooden stairs in the quiet and deserted wing of the building. Debs was still none the wiser why she had unexpectedly been summonsed for a beating but she had no doubt that all would be revealed in the foreseeable future. She twitched her nose and wished Patsy would hurry up.

Patsy Butcher climbed the final flight of stairs that led to the library. At the end of the corridor she could see Deborah standing facing the wall with her hands on her head. The newly appointed Captain of the Red House took a deep breath and strode down the corridor.

Debs didn't move a muscle as she heard the footsteps approaching. The protocols regarding nose and toes were very precise:

1) An inmates nose must be physically touching the wall and toes touching the skirting board throughout a nose and toes session until the release command is issued,

2) At no time during a nose and toes session should an inmate's elbows contact the wall,

3) Contravention of the nose and toes protocols is deemed to be a 'zero tolerance' offence and will be punished with an additional six

strokes to be delivered no earlier than twenty four hours after the primary punishment and no later than thirty-six hours following the contravention.

After four full years at the facility Deborah Morton was fully cognizant with the ramifications of failure to comply with the protocol.

"Lower your arms and follow me, Morton," said Patsy.

Debs and Patsy were tight. Patsy regularly worked out with Deborah, helping her with her short sprints. Patsy's abrupt use of her surname had a jarring effect.

"Yes Ma'am," muttered Deborah as she trudged into the library following the Captain of the Red House.

19

Patsy's First Time Out

The library had an austere atmosphere, lined with shelves filled with dusty books dating back over a century and a half. There were a few areas furnished with tables, inhospitable wooden seated chairs and low-wattage side-lamps. It was many years since the library had been used for its original purpose.

Patsy stopped three quarters of the way along the library. Without needing instruction Deborah continued onwards until she reached a large ornate fireplace that dominated the far wall. She turned around and faced Patsy. Without being asked she reached up and placed her hands on her head.

"You failed to turn up for weeding duty," said Patsy slowly.

Debs gaped at the House Captain. "Weeding duty? I wasn't on the schedule for weeding today," she exclaimed. "I had a clear roster. I checked this morning."

"You were first reserve," said Patsy, sounding uncomfortable. "There were a number of changes to the afternoon duty roster and they were posted before lunch. Unfortunately everybody else checked the notice-board; you were the only one who failed to turn up. The Red House was fined fifteen points so Dame Wharton insists that you are caned."

Deborah grimaced. "I was upstairs studying," she said rather lamely.

"Do you wish to lodge an appeal?" asked Patsy.

Debs licked her dry lips and considered this option. Although the appeal system was designed to offer the inmates a safety net and to dissuade the more tyrannical elements of the Brass and Elite from awarding bogus whops it had a significant downside. An unsuccessful appeal resulted in a second six of the best being delivered twenty-four hours later.

Ms Wharton who served as the Mistress of the Red House was notorious for her strict and often brutal interpretation of the House Protocols. Even if Debs was able to persuade the prefects on the Council of the Red House that it was just an unfortunate oversight the Mistress of the House would still have to sanction the reprieve. From painful experience she knew that in all probability the Wart would interpret her failure to check the notice board as willful negligence or some such nonsense. Unappealing as six might be, one six was certainly preferable to two sixes.

"I'll take a whopping now," she grunted with a decided lack of enthusiasm.

Patsy Butcher took her time taking off her blazer, loosening her collar and rolling back her sleeves. Deborah watched her, her hands still on her head.

Patsy was a beautiful specimen. A five-foot ten inch tall Rastafarian with braided dread-locks that reached down to her waist. Patsy's blouse seemed to have been paint-sprayed to her body and showed off her magnificent physique. Deborah worked out regularly with Patsy and was keenly aware of the strength and power of the House Captains arms.

Patsy picked up the ceremonial Red House cane and swished it through the air.

"I'm going to have to ask you to remove your blazer," she said firmly, "and to bend over and face the fireplace."

Deborah lowered her arms and unfastened the button of her blazer. She shrugged the jacket off and folded it neatly. She turned towards the fireplace.

"Just one more thing, Morton," said Patsy. "I'm afraid this is going to have to be hot. This is my first time out and Ms Wharton is going to need to inspect your stripes. I can't afford to cut you any slack."

"Understood," grunted Deborah and bent forward at the waist until her fingers were resting on the toes of her shoes.

Patsy stepped forward and neatly turned back the hem of Deborah's skirt exposing a drum-tight pair of navy blue gossamer bumbags.

The House Captain tapped the cane down to get her measure, once, twice, thrice and then unleashed a scorcher.

During her certification on the training course Patsy Butcher had demonstrated considerable prowess with the cane. She had been one of the few prefects in the facilities history who had scored perfect marks in every category at her first attempt.

The cane sliced across Deborah's bumbags with the crack of a rifle-shot.

20

A Sensational Swishing

Deborah Morton's backside was a highly-calibrated whopometer and the opening stroke had set alarm bells ringing. The cane had sliced perfectly across the sweet spot of her upturned derriere and had sent a wave of pain ratcheting through Deborah's central nervous system. As she struggled to cope with the blur of pain it occurred to Deborah that if the opener was anything to judge by she was in for an unpleasantly hot and sweaty few minutes.

Patsy had settled into a rhythm. The success of the first stroke had helped to settle her nerves. She favored an eighteen-inch backswing, a smooth approach and relied on the momentum from a last moment flick of the risk to maximize the smart. Upon each impact Deborah's knee's buckled slightly but she resolutely kept her fingers glued to her toes.

Deborah was not having a good time of it. She could take six with the best of them but this was a sensational swishing by any standards. She gritted her teeth as the cane sliced and diced her bumbags with the monotonous rhythm of a metronome.

The position of bending over and touching their toes was extremely unpopular with the inmates. It put considerable strain on the backs of the calves and thighs and was difficult to maintain with a whippy stick rebounding off their bumbags. Of course, like everything else at the Back to School facility, there was a protocol to be followed. The protocol dictated that the victim's fingers must physically be touching her toes throughout the beating. In the event that the victim jerked the stroke could be called foul and repeated.

Deborah was an extraordinarily athletic young woman and physically fit. Under normal circumstances, touching her toes for an extended period of time would not have posed a problem. Nonetheless, even Debs was experiencing difficulties as the cane scorched across her tautened bumbags.

They were five strokes in and Patsy was setting herself up for the closer. Debs ran her tongue over her dry lips. The five stripes were throbbing dreadfully. She felt the cane tapping downwards and then an ominous whistle from behind her.

It took every iota of Deborah's substantial will-power to stay down and not to jerk as the whippy stick sizzled diagonally across the existing stripes. She stared down at the floor, her breath coming in long pants as she felt Patsy turning her skirt back down and then issue the release command. Very slowly Deborah Morton straightened up, her face was pallid and her mouth set in a tight line. Slowly she wriggled across to the side table to retrieve her blazer.

Neither gal spoke during the post-processing. Deborah watched as Patsy fastened her collar and rolled down her sleeves before shrugging on her block red blazer and fastening the five buttons. Debs handed the Captain of the Red House her punishment record book and watched the punishment being added to the new year's tally.

"I'm sorry, Debs," said Patsy, "but I'm going to have to ask you to step up to my study. I'm afraid I wasn't kidding when I said that the Wart wants to inspect your stripes."

Deborah grimaced and followed Patsy towards the door.

The Wart was in rare form. She forced Deborah to bend over the back of the sofa in Patsy's study and took her own sweet time inspecting the House Captain's handiwork. Deborah felt her face turning red as Ms Wharton chuckled and chortled over the vivid red stripes that were visibly pulsating. After she had finished her inspection the Wart cruelly landed two full-blooded spanks across Deborah's twitching buttocks.

"I trust you won't be costing the House any more penalties any time soon," snarled the Wart. "Now straighten up your clothing and get out of my sight. I'm warning you Morton, I'll have my eye on you."

Gloomily Debs reached down and pulled up her bumbags. She smoothed down her skirt and hobbled off in pursuit of Rosemary and her mystical balms.

Later that evening, Debs recorded in her journal, *"Patsy is going to be one to watch. There was an unfortunate misunderstanding over the duty roster and I was summonsed to the library to touch my toes for six. Patsy is definitely a natural, she started well with a real scorcher and slowly worked up to a crescendo. The closer was an absolute cracker and I am still sizzling nearly six hours later."* After a detailed whop by whop description of the beating Deborah concluded with the somewhat rueful observation that, *"I am not having a promising start to the year."*

Nonetheless, despite her unfortunate start to the year Debs Morton had some unfinished business and she was not about to let the small matter of a sore arse get in the way of her plans.

21

Revenge is Not So Sweet

Debs' revenge was not a great success. After lights were turned out for lockdown she had sneaked out of the study she shared with Rosemary Booker and surreptitiously made her way out of the living quarters, across the quadrangle and over to the stables.

Getting the pony out of the stables had proved more difficult than expected. Unlike the more serious equestrians Debs didn't own her own pony so she selected one from the general pool. It had neighed and whinnied so loudly that Debs had almost abandoned the operation at its inception. Deborah had finally managed to pacify the animal with kind words and sugar treats and had eventually succeeded in securing mufflers onto its hooves.

Crossing the quadrangle had been nerve-wracking. She had waited until Sunday night when she figured most of the Brass would be in town, drinking in the local saloon bars. Nonetheless there were still lights in a few of the windows of the floors of the accommodation building occupied by the

Dames. Deborah had gently sweet-talked the pony across the grass, terrified that any second an innocent glance from a lighted window would expose her. Her luck held and she reached the dark safety of the entrance to the science lab. She opened the door and led the pony into the laboratory. She passed through the entrance lobby and went into the chemistry room. Gently she stroked the animal and whispered sweet nothings. She fed it sugar and then laid out some hay at the back of the room and hung a feeding bag around its neck.

She kissed the pony gently. "Be quiet now," she pleaded, "be a good horsy and go to sleep."

The pony appeared to be content to munch on its food. Deborah patted her again and slowly moved away. She backed out of the door, her heart thumping. Suddenly there was an almighty crash of breaking glass and the pony let out an ear-shattering neigh. Deborah's heart missed a beat, she rushed back into the room, the pony neighed again and then promptly dropped her load on the floor. Deborah stared incredulously. She tried to calm the pony's distress but it had worked itself into a frenzy. She had shattered the glass in the front of a cabinet and kicked several stools across the room, making them good for tinder wood.

Deborah's mind was racing. She had to think of something, the cacophony of whinnying and breaking furniture was doubtless audible clear across the quad. The smell of equine defecation was becoming sickening. Deborah snatched up a rag from a sink and blindfolded the pony. Slowly the distressed animal responded to the hapless gal's desperate entreaties. Shaking its head twice and blowing through its nostrils it let out a disgruntled snort and buried its face in the feedbag.

Deborah surveyed the damage and momentarily hung her head.

"Jeepers," she mumbled to herself, "I've really torn it now."

She crossed to the window and peeped out. "Crikey!" she gasped. Phyllis MacAllister, the Science Dame, was bustling across the quadrangle closely followed by Patty Hodge. Apparently they had left the bar early and returned to the compound. Cursing under her breath Deborah frantically raced towards the door. If she was lucky she could escape into the shadows before the two Dames reached the building. As she rushed out she caught sight of the thick leather tawse that hung from a hook beside the blackboard. The mere sight of the dreaded strap gave her supernatural powers and she bounded through the lobby and out into the darkness just moments before the Dames arrived on site.

Deborah stood panting in the shadows. She cautiously peered around the corner of the laboratory building; she knew she had to make a break for it. In a few moments the Dames would be waking up the facility and pursuing the culprit. Deborah shivered, then plucking up her courage she bolted across to the living quarters and slipped through the window that she had left ajar.

She'd only just made it back to the study that she shared with Rosemary before lights went on all over the unit. Hurriedly she changed into her jimjams and slid under the covers. When the light in the room snapped on Deborah feigned sleep. For a second Ms MacAllister stood in the doorway, the fearsome strap in hand. She shut off the light and Deborah breathed a sigh of relief.

22

Prepare for a Flogging

The next morning, Ms Lawton's entrance to the assembly hall was quite formidable. The doors crashed closed behind her and she mounted the steps to the stage two at a time. No sooner had the assembled inmates begun to rise to their feet than they were curtly commanded to sit down. The Grand Dame banged her hand down on the table.

"I want to know who was responsible for the despicable activities in the science block last night," she roared, "I don't care how long it takes but I will find out. Until the culprit comes forward all privileges and recreational activities are canceled for the whole community."

Her face was red with rage and she was visibly shaking as she faced the assembled inmates.

From towards the back of the hall a chair scraped on the wooden floor and the sound of footsteps caused every head in the hall to turn.

Calmly Deborah approached the stage. While the inmates gaped Deborah faced the Grand Dame.

"I'm responsible Ma'am," she said in a clear voice.

Ms Lawton's chin dropped, she simply stared. Her face went from a ruddy flush to a pale haunted color. She was visibly shaken.

"You Morton?" she asked incredulously.

Deborah nodded, "Yes Ma'am" she said firmly.

The Grand Dame breathed heavily, "Go and wait outside my study. I would like to proceed with assembly," she said quietly.

Standing outside the Grand Dame's study, Deborah complimented herself on her composure. When her plan had gone awry she had panicked badly and had sneaked back to bed in a cold sweat. She had hardly been able to sleep, her heart had pounded and her stomach had churned biliously, but as the lonely night had passed she had steadied her nerves and prepared herself to face the inevitable music.

Ms Lawton leaned back in her wing-backed chair and stared thoughtfully at the gal standing before her. Deborah had paid particular attention to her preparations that morning. Her clobber was perfectly pressed, her shoes shone, her face was scrubbed and gleaming, and her mane of blonde curly hair was brushed back from her face and gathered into a tidy pony tail. Standing smartly to attention, in the center of the thick pile carpet, Deborah Morton looked a vision of angelic innocence. Ms Lawton wasn't fooled for a moment.

"It is difficult to know where to begin, Morton," she said slowly. "There must be some explanation for an act of such indescribable vandalism."

Deborah returned the Grand Dame's gimlet glare unflinchingly. "It was a prank, Ma'am."

"A prank, Morton? You leave a terrified pony in the Science lab, expensive equipment has been damaged, the laboratory will be a health hazard for days, and you call it a prank?"

"I didn't mean to scare the pony, Ma'am."

"You take a pony into strange surroundings and you don't think that's cruel?"

"I brought it oats and hay, Ma'am."

The Grand Dame let out a disgusted sigh. She suddenly stood up and leant forward across the desk.

"It was the most stupid, cruel and thoughtless act that I have ever heard of!" she bellowed. "I ought to have you in front of a special parole board this very minute! I could have you put back several years!"

Deborah didn't flinch, "I'm sorry I scared the pony and I'm sorry about the damage, but it was still a prank...Ma'am," she said firmly.

The Grand Dame slammed her hand on the desk. "I'm sure you're sorry now but not half as sorry as you're going to be!" Unflinchingly Deborah continued to stare steadily back at Ms Lawton. Their eyes held for a short moment, the Grand Dame's filled with anger, Deborah's non-committal.

Finally the Grand Dame sat down. Deborah's icy calm was beginning to disconcert her.

Ms Lawton leaned forward in her seat, placed her elbows on the desk and rested her chin on the back of her hands. She breathed deeply. She waited for her fury to subside.

"This is a very difficult situation Morton. You have caused damage to property, incapacitated a laboratory so badly the curriculum has been interrupted, you have caused untold harm to a defenseless pony, not to mention having the whole facility up halfway through the night. Do you understand the seriousness of the trouble you're in?"

Deborah nodded, "Yes Ma'am," she said firmly, "I know that it all looks bad but it was a prank and it all went frightfully wrong."

Ms Lawton picked up the phone. "Katie, come in here. We need to prepare for a flogging."

23

Not Feeling So Lucky

Deborah bent over the vaulting horse. Katie Beck took measurements and then told Debs to stand up. Debs watched morosely as Katie cynically raised the height of the saddle of the horse so that it was at an elevation that would be slightly too high for Deborah to bend over comfortably, and would mean she would have to remain on tiptoes throughout the flogging.

Deborah reached under her skirt and stepped out of her bumbags. She handed them to Katie. The Matron looked at the inside label to find the size. She crossed to a chest of drawers and after rummaging briefly she produced a crisply starched pair of white cotton gym shorts. She handed them to Deborah.
"Put them on," grinned Katie.
Deborah Morton snatched the garment; known to the Woody Wags as whopping bags, and turned her back on Katie. She knew the form. She struggled and squirmed to slide herself into the shorts that

Katie had purposefully selected a size too small. Deborah could barely fasten the button at the waist.

When the bell rang midway through the morning lectures the Woody gals knew what to expect.

"Assemble the inmates," Katie announced over the public address system. "Deborah Morton, Phase 5, twelve stroke public flogging for vandalism."

The announcement that Deborah would receive twelve strokes attracted a lot of raised eyebrows. Public floggings were traditionally divided into two categories.

Mandatory floggings generally related to repeat offenses such as being chucked out of lectures three times during a seven-day period or being chucked out of assembly three times during a single term. Mandatory floggings were carried out during Callover and were limited to six strokes of the senior cane.

Punishment floggings were administered for more serious offenses that included cussing out the Brass or the Elite, smoking, boozing, scrapping or cutting curfew. At any time day or night the inmates could be summonsed to the assembly hall to witness a punishment flogging which was comprised of nine strokes.

A twelve-stroke flogging was unprecedented and the news was not well received by the inmates of the facility.

"Bummer! Twelve strokes is a bit strong," grumbled Nix as she and her chums strode towards the assembly hall.

"Tough duty," agreed Jojo. "Still it could have been worse, she could have been sent up before a parole board."

"Thank heavens for small mercies," sighed Rosemary.

Debs Morton was not thanking anyone for small mercies. Ms Lawton had Deborah pinned down over her knee, with her white cotton whopping bags rolled down and concertinaed around her ankles. Ms Lawton was giving Debs a damn good spanking. Debs had reluctantly allowed herself to be lowered downwards and stretched out into the mandatory full drape so that she was fully supported by Ms Lawton with only the tips of her fingers and her toes touching the carpet.

However much she hated being hand spanked like a grubby Deborah was forced to grudgingly admit that the warm-up actually helped her to get into the zone. Being caned in front of the whole unit was always a daunting experience but as a fully paid up mega-minx Deborah was duty bound to take her flogging without making a muff of herself.

Ms Lawton pulled Deborah in tight and Debs settled in for a few very hot and very sweaty minutes.

Debs pulled up the zip and fastened the button on the side of her shorts. The material chaffed against the swollen flesh. She wriggled involuntarily. Over the intercom she heard Katie summonsing the inmates to the assembly hall. She felt a shiver up her spine.

Ms Lawton was at the tall-boy selecting a cane, flexing them between her hands and swishing them through the air until she found one to her liking.

"You can consider yourself lucky that I haven't sent you before a disciplinary hearing," she told Deborah coldly, "but I can assure you Morton, I intend to flog you with the utmost severity."

"Yes, Ma'am," said Deborah, although she wasn't too sure that she was exactly feeling lucky.

24

Bend Over the Horse!

The Grand Dame held the door for Deborah and they entered the Assembly Hall. There was a grinding of seats as the inmates rose to acknowledge the arrival of the Grand Dame. Deborah stepped up onto the stage and stood beside the vaulting horse. She clasped her hands in front of her and gazed out over the assembled congregation. The Grand Dame ordered the inmates to take their seats and unhurriedly she asked Penelope Ann Evans to step onto the stage and call registration.

As she passed by Deborah, Penelope Ann threw her a sympathetic glance; Debs winked. The Red-shirt called registration efficiently and when she called Deborah's name the gal on the stage turned to face her and replied in a voice filled with irony, "Yes, Evans, I'm here."

Even the Grand Dame grinned at that.

Finally the Red-shirt returned to her place by the wall and the Grand Dame stood up. She moved to the front of the stage and addressed the inmates. She admonished Deborah's behavior savagely and informed the assembled inmates of her intention to punish Debs extremely soundly. During the speech Deborah was pulling sarcastic faces at the gals who sat before her. They began to chuckle and were immediately silenced by the Grand Dame but when she turned suspiciously to look at her Deborah's expression was one of stony indifference.

Ms Lawton slipped off her black double-breasted jacket and hung it up. She was wearing a white silk blouse with the collar turned up at the back. She unfastened the cuffs and neatly rolled back her sleeves to below the elbow. Deborah watched with stony-faced resignation. She was keenly aware that in a matter of moments the fireworks were scheduled to begin.

When the Grand Dame turned to collect the long thin senior cane from the table Deborah spotted her chum Rosemary waving crossed fingers from the back of the hall; Deborah winked again. The inmates chuckled behind their hands. If the Grand Dame was aware of Deborah's performance she chose to ignore it.

She took the long crook-handled cane from the table and turned to face her victim. She held the long thin cane between both hands and flexed it into an arc.

"Bend over the horse," she instructed.

Deborah turned and faced the vaulting horse. Due to the extra three inches that Katie had raised the saddle Debs had to tiptoe up as she bent forward at the waist. She reached down and gripped the legs on the far side, her hips rested on the top of the horse; she was balanced on the tips of her toes.

The inmates were treated to the sight of Deborah's bottom, shrouded in the skintight white whopping bags with razor vertical creases, as it sat up proud and defenseless.

The Grand Dame stood to the left of Deborah and placed the cane on the upturned moons and tapped the stick down gently to gauge her distance. The tight gym shorts made Deborah's slightly plump rump an especially enticing target. She tapped the cane down a second time and then a third.

Deborah closed her eyes tightly.

Satisfied, Ms Lawton pulled her arm back, cocked ready for release. With a look of rapt concentration on her face she swiped the cane downwards with extreme prejudice. The cane sliced through the air with a sharp whistle and rebounded off Deborah's backside with a resounding crack.

Deborah felt the breath knocked from her and she held onto the legs with a vice-like grip. A line of scalding fire flashed across her tender behind. If the opener was anything to go by Deborah was about to experience an exceptionally painful few minutes.

The seasoned veterans in the hall watched closely. Although the Grand Dames back-swing was deceptively short there was no question that she had opened with a scorcher. The inmates exchanged knowing glances. It was clear that Ms Lawton intended to teach Deborah a lesson that she wasn't likely to forget in a hurry.

The cane swished and thwacked again; Deborah felt as if every nerve end in her body had been sent into a hot prickly dance. The third slashed downwards and the hapless Debs felt giddy with pain. The collar of her blouse felt like it was choking her and her eyes prickled with hot tears that she would never let fall.

The Beak delivered stroke after stroke with deadly force. By the seventh stroke Deborah's buttocks were evenly covered with hot stripes from top to bottom. The eighth and ninth strokes began to merge with the existing stripes but somehow Deborah retained her position without moving and was showing no indication of the trauma she was suffering. Ms Lawton felt cheated; she was giving it her best and was getting no reaction. She set her mouth in a determined manner and took a tight grip on the cane.

"Let's see how you like this," the Grand Dame thought silently then raised the cane slightly higher than usual and brought her arm down with considerable force. The cane slashed across the target with a terrible crack, as if a rifle shot had been fired.

25

Snap Goes Beaky's Cane

Deborah's head was spinning. The flesh beneath her crisp white whopping bags seemed to be sizzling. She shook her head in a desperate attempt to clear the fog of pain. "It's only whops, it's only whops," she repeated over and over. Somewhere in the distance she heard an audible gasp.

The Grand Dame stared at the cane in horror; upon its devastating impact the shaft of the cane had snapped off at the end. For a moment Ms Lawton was at a loss as how to proceed. During decades of thrashing thousands of luckless behinds she had never once broken a cane. It had never occurred to her that she might need a back-up. Clearly there was no time to send for another cane from her office, she couldn't leave Deborah folded over the horse. Her mind raced.

"Melanie, bring me your ashplant," she commanded. Quickly the Deputy Red-shirt came onto the stage and handed the Grand Dame the short swishy stick that she was required to carry under her arm at all times.

Deborah had no idea what was going on she just wanted the last two strokes to be over with. Her bottom felt fried and frazzled, all her blood seemed to have rushed to her head making her feel dizzy.

The Grand Dame flexed the ashplant with obvious displeasure. The light rod seemed like a mere twig compared to the regal senior cane that now lay cast aside, pathetically broken.

"I'm sorry Morton," she announced. "This ashplant is most unsuitable; I intend to give you two additional strokes to make up for its inadequacy."

The inmates gasped audibly. Deborah, in her upside down position, could hardly believe her ears. She vainly tried to object but before she could get words of her mouth her arse was under fire once again. Deborah's head was spinning at an alarming rate as the twelfth stroke whistled through the air. She clenched her teeth as the nerve jangling implosion racked through her body. The thirteenth stroke followed swiftly with the same cobra's venom. Deborah gripped the legs of the horse in white-knuckle desperation. By now she could hardly breathe through the bile filling her throat and nose and her bottom throbbed and ached and burned.

The Grand Dame let the cane fall by her side for a moment. She studied the white target thoughtfully. Deborah had not flinched or moved, not a sound had uttered from her lips. Ms Lawton was sure that if she put her hands close to the gal's backside she would be able to warm them as if she was in front of a well-stoked coal fire. The Grand Dame lifted the cane for the final time.

The gals in the assembly hall watched in mute horror as the Grand Dame's arm went up. Most of the gals congregated had experienced a taste of a prefect's ashplant during their stay at Woodys. As such they were well able to confirm that, despite the Grand Dame's reservations, the ashplant, in accomplished hands was more than adequate to stir up the proverbial hornet's nest inside a pair of tautened bumbags

When the ashplant came down with a terrific swipe not a single gal in the hall would have swapped places in Deborah's gym shorts. The stick lashed diagonally across Deborah's bottom, cruelly crossing each of the previous tramlines, the impact echoing around the hall.

Deborah nearly screamed. She wanted to howl, to yell, to open the floodgates and let all the tears burn down her cheeks. Instead she held her breath and prayed that the wave of agony would pass quickly. She ran the sleeve of her blouse over her eyes and nose. She hung upside down and tried to start to breathe normally. She took her time before she pushed herself up. As she tried to stand up her knees wobbled and Ms Lawton put her hand on her shoulder to steady her. Deborah Morton roughly shrugged the Grand Dame's assistance away and leant against the vaulting horse. She took a deep breath before she turned and faced the audience.

The hall was silent. Every gal was watching Deborah in disbelieving silence. Despite her chalk white face and the thin set of her lips, she remained defiant. She brushed some hair from her face, tucked her tie back in her gym shorts and calmly stared out at the assembled inmates.

"You may retire to your study now Morton," the Grand Dame told Deborah curtly. "We'll post-process you later."

The recalcitrant inmate looked at the Grand Dame contemptuously. "You wanted to thrash me, well now you have. I hope you enjoyed it," her voice was clear and bold. When she had finished speaking she turned on her heel and walked towards the steps. Suddenly she turned around and curtsied.

"Thank you Ma'am," she said sarcastically, "You won't have to beat me like that again."

As she hurried from the stage her heart was pounding and her bottom felt like a cauldron filled with spicy ingredients each competing for which could make the gumbo hottest. All the while she was waiting to be called back, but in a moment the doors of the hall were swinging behind her and to her great relief she was free.

26

Operation Scorched Arse

Freedom, however, was short lived. Later that evening Cassandra Cassidy hurried into the study that Joanna Heyworth shared with Nicola Jane Nixon. She told them that her sister, Cathryn, urgently needed to see them, and was waiting behind the stables. They were to bring Debs and Rosemary and not to tell anyone else or let anybody see them.

The four chums were curious about the clandestine request but they knew that if Cat Cassidy saw the need for secrecy then they had better comply. They hurried down the back stairs and cut across the quadrangle.

When the chums arrived at the stables, Cathryn was waiting with Lady Victoria Brompton and Claire Brooks.

"What's all the secrecy, Cat?" asked Jojo.

Cathryn hushed her. For once the imperturbable Cat looked cagey and anxious.

"Look, I really don't want to get caught talking to you while I'm wearing these bumbags. The Beak warned us that if we let the cat out of the bag we'd be flogged," she said earnestly, "So hush up and listen."

Cathryn dispatched her younger sister, Cassie Cassy, to wait by the doors and keep watch.

Cathryn Cassidy told her chums that immediately after Deb's flogging the Grand Dame had summoned the Brass and the Elite to an emergency summit.

At the meeting the Grand Dame had announced that she was rolling out a program of Radical Revisions to the rules, regulations and protocols. Cat told her chums that the details were sketchy but the Brass and the Elite had been instructed to implement a zero-tolerance policy with immediate effect. The new program was to be code-named Operation Scorched Arse.

Cat told her chums that the Grand Dame had only had time to give a brief overview of the revisions but she had handed out thick files for the Brass and Elite to read.

Nonetheless, said Cat, even without studying the details the signs were ominous; Ms Lawton had declared open season on mega-minxdom.

She had nominated twelve gals to be treated as hostiles, and had branded them the Dirty Dozen. Cathryn showed them a copy of a presentation slide that had been distributed at the meeting:

The Dirty Dozen

Code : Red
Priority : High
Implementation : Immediate
Eyes Only : Brass and Elite

Name	Phase	Hostility Ranking
Extreme Prejudice		
Deborah Morton	5	1*
Lisa Sutton	4	2**
Zero Tolerance		
Joanna Heyworth	5	3
Lady Victoria Brompton	6	4
Bernadette Summers	4	5
Claire Brooks	6	6
Nicola Jane Nixon	5	7
Rosemary Booker	5	8
Cassandra Cassidy	2	9
Julie Beckett	3	10
Ali Stone	5	11
Rachel Cox	6	12

* Morton is officially classified as Public Enemy Number One. She is to be targeted as a Hostile and treated with Extreme Prejudice.
** Sutton will be de-classified to Public Enemy Number Two, however, Hostile Targeting should continue.

"Good fucking grief," said Jojo.

"Good fucking grief indeed," Cat sighed. "Listen sisters, I can't hang about. If we get caught gabbing about this it'll be whops for all of us. Just be careful sisters, cos you're in for some surprises. Spread the word and cover your bumbags because the Brass and the Elite are coming in whopping."

With that Cathryn Cassidy, the original architect of the lifestyle of mega-minxdom, slipped into the night.

"Operation Scorched Arse, what does that mean?" asked Cassie Cassy.

Lady Victoria Brompton scowled, "Declaration of war on our bumbags is what it means," she said emphatically.

"Sounds like something the CIA would dream up," growled Nixdown.

Debs Morton looked gloomy. "Public Enemy Number One? Why the fuck has she picked on me?"

"Oh put your bumbags in it Debs," said Nix cynically. "You'll love the attention."

Deborah glared at Nix.

"I think this means we're in for a long, hot winter," predicted Jojo Heyworth.

27

Miss Deborah Morton

Unfortunately for Debs it was not the first time in her life that she had found herself branded as a hostile and singled out for prejudicial treatment.

Unlike Joanna, whose school had not practiced corporal punishment; Deborah Morton had a long acquaintance with the cane. Her mother had been a former pupil of the original Woody School and when her alma mater had closed down she had sought out a boarding school that was run on equally strict disciplinary principles. Deborah was dispatched to the Queensgate Academy for Young Ladies.

At Queensgate Debs would gain a reputation as an academic wunderkind, she was selected to play clarinet with the National Youth Orchestra, and quickly rose to fame as the number one female tennis player in the country.

However, a review of the school's punishment record book demonstrates that all that's gold does not always glitter.

During her first three years at the school she also gained a reputation as an unruly pupil. The school teaching staff was far too genteel to actually punish the students and operated a system where undisciplined pupils were 'Put on the Menu'. Girls on the menu were required to report before the school's prefectorial body known as the Posh. After being charged the miscreants were given the opportunity to either plead guilty as charged, make a plea bargain to a lesser charge, or to defend themselves. The Posh had a variety of punishments at their disposal including lines, detentions, community service and the elimination of privileges. They were also permitted to sentence girls to be thrashed with a ceremonial cane known as the 'popping stick'.

Deborah appeared on the menu with increasing frequency and despite her reputation as a skilled and articulate advocate in her own defense she was thrashed twenty-five times during her first three years at the academy.

Her fourth year was a catastrophe with her behavior spiraling out of control and she made a record-breaking number of appearances on the menu. Despite her silver tongue and deft defenses the odds were stacked against her and predictably she established another record receiving nineteen beatings during the period. Coincidentally the President of Posh who was responsible for administering the thrashings was Pauline Gascoigne who would later take on the role of Economics Dame at the Woody Back to School Unit.

This pattern of misbehavior caused the Principal of the academy to take extreme action. Deborah was summonsed to the Great House for a personal interview the Grand Dame. This in itself was unprecedented. The Grand Dame lived in isolation from the main school leaving administration and discipline to the twenty-one members of the Posh.

During the interview the Grand Dame showed Debs her end of year report card. At the bottom of the card there was a section for the Grand Dame to assign a cumulative grade for academics, sporting achievement and behavior. Grading was scaled between A and E. In the first two boxes Deborah had been graded A+ for her schoolwork and her performance at sports. However, in the behavior box the Grand Dame had crossed through the scores and simply written DEPLORABLE in red ink.

Deborah was informed that during the forthcoming school year she would be required to carry a special book with her at all times and at the end of each class she would present it to the presiding Dame to have her behavior graded. She would no longer be placed on the menu by the Dames which at least would have given her the opportunity to defend herself. Instead, she was informed, in the event that she scored three grades of C- or less during any given week she would receive a mandatory beating on Friday evening.

Foolishly Deborah continued to flirt with fate and during the first week following her return to school she accumulated three bad grades. The Grand Dame sentenced her to six strokes of the cane. In the ensuing weeks she continued to fail to meet the performance criteria and each week her punishment was increased by an additional stroke. By the end of the fourth week she was sentenced to the maximum dosage of nine strokes and was warned that she would continue to get nine until she succeeded in getting through a week with acceptable behavior grades.

By the time she left the academy to play on the professional tennis circuit Deborah Morton had been beaten on thirty-nine consecutive Fridays.

An examination of the national archive of the Ministry of Education dating back over one hundred and fifty years reveals that with an accumulation of eighty-three beatings Miss Deborah Morton holds the record for being caned more than any other school pupil in recorded history.

Debs Morton slipped under her duvet. The stripes on her backside were still sizzling like sausages in a pan filled with oil. She had an uncomfortable premonition that life was about to become even hotter inside her already poor beleaguered bumbags. She sighed and turned off the side-light.